ABOUT THIS BOOK

**From *USA Today* bestselling author Apryl Baker . . . A single
random act. One swerve of a car. In a blink, it's all gone.**
    Cora Hartwood lost everything in a single heartbeat, and she's
left with crushing guilt and dark thoughts that drive her to consider
even darker ideas. She and her grandmother came to Havenwood
Falls for a new start, to get away from the memories of the tragedy
that took her family.
    Or so she thought.
    Her grandmother reveals that what happened to her family
wasn't an accident. They were murdered, and the two of them fled
to Havenwood Falls and the safety it offered. The secrets of her
family's past are revealed, leaving Cora to question everything.
    Now she's not only dealing with guilt, but she worries about
becoming a victim to the same person who took her family from
her. She's scared and falling apart.
    Until she meets Reed Spencer.
    He seems to understand the dark place she's in and brings a
little light into her life. He's the one person she can turn to, and he's
quickly becoming not only her friend, but something more.
    But she's not as safe as she thinks, and it will take the magic of
Havenwood Falls to save her.

HAVENWOOD FALLS HIGH BOOKS

Written in the Stars by Kallie Ross

Reawakened by Morgan Wylie

The Fall by Kristen Yard

Somewhere Within by Amy Hale

Awaken the Soul by Michele G. Miller

Bound by Shadows by Cameo Renae

Fata Morgana by E.J. Fechenda

Forever Emeline by Katie M. John

Reclamation by AnnaLisa Grant

Avenoir by Daniele Lanzarotta

Avenge the Heart by Michele G. Miller

Curse the Night by R.K. Ryals

Blood & Iron by Amy Hale

Shadows & Spells by Cameo Renae

Falling Deep by J.L. Weil

Saving Infiniti by Rose Garcia

Willful by Liz Ferry

Cast in Moonlight by Ali Winters

Promise the Moon by Kallie Ross

Blurred Lines by Daniele Lanzarotta

Ascending Darkness by J.L. Weil

Finding Infiniti by Rose Garcia

Unicorn's Lament by Megan Linski

Paper Bird by Amy Richie

Predestined by Valia Lind

Rediscovered by Morgan Wylie

Ashes of Fate by Apryl Baker

Stay up to date at www.HavenwoodFalls.com

BOOKS BY APRYL BAKER

The Ghost Files Series

The Ghost Files

The Ghost Files V2

The Ghost Files V3

The Ghost Files V3.5

The Ghost Files V4.1

The Ghost Files V4.2

The Ghost Files V5

Silas (A Ghost Files Novella)

The Crane Diaries Series

The Crane Diaries: Homecoming

The Crane Diaries: Dirty Blood

The Crane Diaries: Stained

The Crane Diaries: The Red Church

The Crane Diaries: Bayou Secrets

The Bloodlines Legacy Series

The Blackburne Legacy

The Blackwater Legacy

The Blackstone Legacy

The Manwhore Series

Touch Me Not

The Sinner's Touch

The Healing Touch

Forever Your Touch

Kincaid Security & Investigation Series

Kade

Viktor

Mason

Jasper

The DeCadia Series

The DeCadia Code

The Crucible

Destiny's End

The Invasion Series

The Invasion

Fight Back

Stand Your Ground

Hybrid

ASHES OF FATE

APRYL BAKER

For my sister Joannie, who has risen from the ashes more than once this year.

CHAPTER 1

CHARLESTON, SC

"*C*ora!"

Cora Hartwood ignored her best friend's shout, instead focusing on the super cute Dracula sitting beside her. Seth Michaels had been flirting with her for three days and she'd finally worked up the courage to pull him into a semi-quiet corner of the biggest party of the year. Bonfires raged along the beach outside, but she'd never liked fire and chose to stay indoors.

Most everyone was out there, and she and Seth could cuddle and maybe make out a little. At least that was the plan, if Emily would shut up.

"You look hot as a zombie nurse," Seth whispered in Cora's ear, his teeth tugging at her earlobe. She shivered in response, loving the way he made her feel. Cora had made out with a couple guys before, but none of them gave her butterflies in her stomach like Seth did.

"You don't look so bad yourself, Count Dracula." Cora giggled and leaned in closer, snuggling up to Seth.

"Cora Jean Hartwood!"

The sheer desperation in Emily's voice startled her into looking away from Seth, her gaze finding Emily in a few seconds. She looked scared.

Cora pushed up from Seth, who called after her, and went running.

"What is it?" She grasped Emily's arm and pulled her friend around to face her. "Are you okay? Did somebody try something? Just tell me who and I'll . . ."

"No, not me!" Emily's dark brown eyes were wide with so many different emotions, Cora couldn't keep up. "The sheriff's here looking for you."

"Me?" Shock rippled through her. She'd been with some friends earlier but had left before they'd started to egg cars and houses. Surely someone hadn't called and reported her for hanging with them, making the sheriff think she was a part of that nonsense.

"Something happened, Cora, something bad. You need to come with me."

She refused to budge, a knot of fear beginning to twist in her stomach. "Tell me what's wrong."

"I . . . I don't know. Sheriff McCarty wouldn't say. He just said to find you and bring you out front."

"Cora?" Seth came to a stop beside her. "What's going on?"

"I don't know, but I have to go." She didn't even look at him, but followed Emily out of the beach house, her mind sorting through a million different what-ifs. The waves were crashing onto the sand, coming close to the bonfires, which blazed high. The fire held her attention for a brief moment. She hated fire, and right now, it seemed to mock her, to tease her that it was about to rob her of everything precious.

Shivering, she turned away and followed Emily down to where the sheriff's SUV was parked at the very edge of the property. He looked grim.

"Sheriff, this is Cora." Emily grabbed Cora's hand and held tight.

"Miss Hartwood, there's been an accident."

"Accident?" A new kind of fear curled in her stomach, and she got very, very cautious. "What kind of accident?"

"Your parents and brother were involved in a motor vehicle accident this evening. They've all been rushed to the hospital in critical condition."

Motor vehicle accident.

Her mind went blank, and she felt numb. The chill in the air disappeared as well as all the sounds around her. Emily's and the sheriff's faces faded away as those three little words swirled round and round in her head.

"Cora!"

Hands grabbed her as her body sagged. Her family was in an accident while she'd been making out at a party. She was supposed to have gone with them to the pumpkin patch and then to the haunted house in town. But she'd decided to go hang out with her friends instead.

She was supposed to have been in that car.

"Miss Hartwood?"

She blinked, her mind refocusing on the sheriff. "They're not dead?"

"I won't lie. It doesn't look good. We need to get you to the ER if you want to see them."

Cora nodded and took out her phone, texting her grandma. She lived in Florida, but she would find a way to get here. Cora only saw her grandma at Christmas, and they Skyped on birthdays, but despite not being as close as they could be, Hattie should know.

And Cora needed her.

Emily climbed into the back of the SUV with her, but Cora was barely aware of her. She kept thinking about her family. Her little brother had begged her to come with them, but she'd wanted to go to the party where all her friends were. She wanted to hang out with Seth instead of Billy. If she'd just been in the backseat of her parents' car, maybe she could have shielded Billy. Maybe he wouldn't have gotten hurt.

Emily snapped her fingers in front of Cora's face, bringing her out of her haze. "Your phone's ringing."

Cora stared at it. Her grandmother's face was on the screen. Even though she'd texted her a few minutes ago, she couldn't bring herself to answer it. That would mean admitting out loud how bad the situation was.

Emily took the phone from her and answered it, explaining everything to her grandmother. Cora heard her, but it was like she was hearing her from the end of a long tunnel.

Shock. This had to be shock. Her body was in shock.

But she couldn't do anything to help herself.

"Cora, your grandmother said to tell you she'll be on the first flight she can get."

Cora nodded, her fingers twisting each other. Emily pulled her hands apart. "You're going to hurt yourself."

They rode in silence for the rest of the way, and when the sheriff pulled up in front of the ER, Cora's body refused to move. Emily sat with her and eventually coaxed her out, but a fear unlike anything she'd ever known crept up and took a hold of her.

Walking through the ER doors, she all but stopped breathing, holding onto Emily's hand so tightly, the circulation might have been cut off. The girls followed the sheriff to the information desk. The nurse looked over at her, her expression sympathetic and full of pity.

Cora's heart sank.

There would be no reason she'd give her that look unless it was bad. How bad remained to be seen.

They were escorted into the ER itself and into a small waiting area. A few other people were there, but they were told a doctor would be out to see them shortly.

"Wha . . . what happened? Can you tell me?"

"It looks like a hit and run," the sheriff said. "There was a witness to the accident who called 9-1-1. The car in front of the witness was going really fast and swerved into your parents' lane.

They hit your family head on. The witness said it looked like your father lost control and spun out, slamming into the guard rail, and flipped, forcing the car over the rail and into the ravine. We have an APB out with the car's description and the partial plate number the witness was able to provide."

Cora nodded. A random act. One swerve and it cost her family so much.

A man wearing scrubs came out a few minutes later. He walked straight to her, his expression kind. "Miss Hartwood?"

"Yes." Cora stood, still clutching Emily's hand like a lifeline.

"I'm Dr. Hall. We've got your parents stable, but they both need surgery. I need you to sign a consent since you're the next of kin."

"My gran is on her way. She's getting the first flight out."

"We don't have time to wait. If we don't operate now, they'll die."

"They'll live if you do?" Cora whispers.

"I can't promise you that. Their injuries are severe, but surgery is their best option."

"And my brother?"

"I'm sorry. He died before he got to the hospital."

"No." Cora didn't recognize the sound that escaped her. It was a half cry, half moan. Her knees weakened, and she sank back down.

"I'm very sorry," the doctor said. "I hate to ask this of you, but we need to go now if we're going to save them."

Why would they ask her to do this? It wasn't fair. She was only seventeen. She shouldn't have to make this decision.

"Miss Hartwood?" the doctor prompted when she didn't answer.

"Okay. Please, just don't let them die. Please."

Papers were handed to her, and she signed them blindly.

"Can I see them before you go into surgery?"

"I'm afraid not. We need to get them into surgery now."

Again, she nodded and watched the doctor walk away.

Emily squeezed her hand. "It's going to be okay, Cora."

"It's not. Billy died. My brother died." Tears started leaking, and once the waterworks began, they wouldn't stop.

Emily hugged her close, whispering things Cora didn't hear.

All she could think about was her brother and her parents as they sat and waited for the doctor to come back.

CHAPTER 2

*C*ora shifted in her seat for the thousandth time. She and her grandmother had been on the road for three days, taking turns driving so they'd get to Colorado faster. Not that Cora cared. Her family was gone in a car accident she should have been in. It wasn't fair that she lived and they all died.

"We're almost there, I think." Hattie looked at the directions she had written down. The GPS had stopped working about an hour ago, much to Cora's disgust.

"I don't know, Gran. I think we're lost."

"We're not lost." Hattie folded up the map and pointed to the McDonald's building up ahead. "That's where we're supposed to wait for the bus we'll follow into Havenwood Falls. See the advertisement for it?"

"The GPS . . ."

"The mountains block the GPS signal."

It sounded perfectly reasonable, but somehow Cora didn't quite believe that. Even in the mountains there should be areas where a signal came through, not this wasteland. Even her cell had no signal.

"I still don't know why we have to move here. Why couldn't you stay in Charleston or I could have come to Florida?"

"I promised you I'd explain everything once we reached Havenwood Falls."

"Well, we're here, so why not tell me while we wait?" Cora pulled into the parking lot, but she didn't cut the engine. Why did Gran have to move them somewhere cold? She was a beach girl, not a snow bunny.

"Why don't we go to the restroom instead? Once we're settled in, I'll sit you down and explain why we had to run."

"Run?" Cora asked, alarmed. "What are you talking about, Gran?"

"It's complicated, and now is not the time to discuss it."

"Now is the perfect time to discuss it. What did you mean we had to run?"

Gran pursed her lips. "What happened to your family wasn't an accident."

"But the police said . . . there was a drunk driver . . ." What the heck was her gran talking about?

Gran shook her head. "I'll explain when we get inside the boundaries of Havenwood Falls. You're going to have to trust me, Cora. Now, let's go use the restroom and grab something to eat."

Cora stared openmouthed as her gran got out of the car and went into the McDonald's. Her mind buzzed with a thousand questions, but she knew her grandmother well enough to know she wasn't going to budge. Cora got out and locked the car. She did need to go to the bathroom.

Unfortunately, she had no coat. Her clothes were not meant for the mountains of Colorado. So she froze her butt off all the way into the fast-food restaurant. Shivering, she found the bathroom and saw her gran's feet under one of the stalls. She quickly did her business and washed her hands.

"Gran, you okay in there?"

"I'm old. I take longer to pee than you do. It comes out in . . ."

"Not what I want to hear!" she cut Hattie off. *Eww. Just gross.*

Hattie chuckled and slid her purse out from under the stall

door. "Go get us some food. I want two Big Macs. They have that buy-one-get-one-free deal going on right now."

"You're really going to eat two of those things? Do you know how much fat is in just one?"

"I sure do, but at my age, I don't care. And I want a strawberry milkshake."

"Heart attack waiting to happen," Cora muttered, then stopped short, realizing what she'd said. "Gran, maybe you should . . ."

"I'm not going anywhere. Got my ticker checked two weeks ago, and it's in perfect working order. Don't worry about me, sweetheart. The reaper is going to have a fight on his hands should he come knocking at my door. That I promise."

Cora nodded and went out to order the food. She decided to go back to the car after she'd gotten their food because she wasn't sure when the bus was supposed to show up that they'd follow all the way to Havenwood Falls.

Havenwood Falls. She shook her head as she hurried back to the car. It sounded like the title of a romance novel. Her mom used to love to read paranormal romances. The ache in her chest worsened at the thought of her mother, and her breathing sped up. Her hands started to shake, and she all but ran to the safety of the vehicle and the duffel bag on the back seat.

She dug out her anxiety medication and took one. She hated these things, but they helped with the panic attacks she'd been experiencing since the night her family died. Her doctor thought it was due to how much guilt she carried for not being in the car with them. He was probably right, but she didn't know what to do about it. Her gran had mentioned finding someone for her to talk to once they were in Havenwood Falls, but she wasn't sure how she felt about that.

She sat behind the wheel and took deep breaths, trying to calm down. She tried counting while she waited for the medicine to start to work, but it wasn't until her gran came back and started to talk to her that her nerves began to settle.

"Easy, Bug, it's all going to be okay. Everything will be fine. Just take deep breaths."

Bug. Only Gran ever called her that. It was so far from the nickname her parents used, it actually helped to take away some of the panic.

"There's my girl."

"I . . . I'm sorry . . . I . . ."

"Shh, nothing to be sorry about, Bug-a-boo. Swap seats with me, and I'll drive the rest of the way. You took one of your pills?"

Cora nodded and switched seats. The medicine didn't state she couldn't drive, but neither of them were willing to take the chance on another accident.

Hattie opened the bag and handed Cora her chicken nuggets. "I spoke with Greg. He's got both shops packed up, and the boxes are en route to Havenwood Falls. I've already applied for a business license, so we should have the toy shop up and running before Black Friday."

The family toy shop. The Hartwoods had been making toys for over two hundred years. She wasn't sure she wanted anything to do with it now that her family was gone, though.

"The building I'm looking at has enough room for a candy store as well. Your dad said you'd started making candy for the store there, so I thought maybe we could expand on it, have a huge shop. They already have a sweets shop with ice cream and things, but no one makes homemade candies."

"I don't know, Gran, after everything . . ."

"You think about it. It's not like we have to decide right this second. Once we get there and have a look around, we'll talk about it again."

"There wouldn't be time if you want to open by Thanksgiving. It's only three weeks away. I'm not even sure you can be open even with all the stock arriving on time. There's signage and remodeling . . ."

"It'll be open even if I have to work twenty-four hours a day. It'll give me something to do."

The hollowness in her grandmother's voice reminded Cora she wasn't the only one who'd lost family. Hattie lost her son, daughter-in-law, and grandson too. She was in just as much pain as Cora. Getting the toy store together would probably help her to heal. Maybe it could help Cora too.

"We'll get it open, Gran. Let's just hope they have a good construction company that doesn't mind working long days and maybe nights too."

Her grandmother bit into her Big Mac and all but moaned out loud. She reminded Cora more of a teenager than a sixty-year-old woman. Then again, with the streaks of blue hair running through her white locks and the big white sunglasses she had on, she looked more like a teenager than a grandmother.

Cora's own hair was blond with strips of purple and pink running through it. She loved her hair, so who was she to frown on Hattie for being un-grandmotherly?

"We need to get a coat somewhere." Cora dunked a nugget into honey mustard sauce. "I almost froze my butt off going inside."

"It's not that cold." Hattie sat her burger down and took a long pull of her milkshake.

"According to the radio, it's in the low forties. Forties, Gran!"

Hattie grimaced. "Well, maybe it's a little colder than we're used to. I'm sure they have a store there where we can buy some warm clothes and a coat."

"Is that the bus?" Cora pointed to the large bus that had just pulled up.

Hattie looked at her Big Mac longingly. "Yes. Don't you see the Havenwood Falls logo?"

"You'd better eat up then. I doubt they'll be here long."

Hattie wasted no time in consuming her burger. It amazed Cora someone as tiny as her grandmother could eat like she did.

"Feeling better now?" Hattie asked after a few minutes.

"Yeah. I'm tired, though."

"Get some sleep, Bug-a-boo, and when you wake up, we'll be in our new home."

Cora wasn't so sure about calling it home yet, but she was tired and fell asleep before the bus they'd follow pulled out.

CHAPTER 3

Cora blinked bleary eyes open when her grandmother shook her awake. It was pitch dark outside, so she must have slept for longer than she intended.

Hattie motioned out the windshield. "Look, you can see the lights of the town."

Dutifully, she looked, and sure enough, the town was laid out before her in a maze of lights. It looked pretty, nestled against the mountains. Snow always looked pretty in pictures, though she herself had very little opportunity to see it up close and personal. She had a feeling she was going to get the opportunity to see more than her fair share in this quaint little mountain town.

They drove through several streets and then turned down another street. Hattie came to a stop at Whisper Falls Inn, an old Victorian mansion. It was just as beautiful as the rest of the town. She and her grandmother got out of the car and hurried inside.

A young woman was behind the front desk and smiled warmly when she saw the two of them approaching. "Welcome to Whisper Falls Inn."

"Yes, I spoke with someone earlier about a late check in. I'm Hattie Hartwood."

"Ah, yes, I heard you were opening a toy shop here in town."

"More like relocating our existing stores to here," Hattie said and shifted from foot to foot. She looked tired. Cora should have driven, even though she'd taken her anxiety meds. Her grandmother was getting on in years, even if she didn't look a day over fifty.

"Well, it will be a welcome addition, I'm sure."

They both turned to see a young woman come striding toward them, another pleasant smile plastered on her face. "I'm Michaela Petran, and I wanted to welcome you to our town. We're all very excited to have you here."

"I wasn't aware everyone knew we were coming," Hattie said dryly.

"Well, Saundra happened to mention it to a few people."

"Saundra?" Cora whispered to her grandmother.

"Saundra Beaumont." Hattie turned toward Cora. "She and I are old friends, and when she heard what happened, she offered us a place to stay here in town. She even found a location for the new store and got the paperwork started for us."

"Handcrafted toys are going to be a big hit with the tourists," Michaela went on. "And she said something about homemade candy too. I have a sweet tooth, so I'm hoping you'll be able to open the store soon."

"My goal is to have it open for Black Friday. I just need to hire a construction crew that's fast and reliable and won't overcharge me."

"I can help you out with that, but that can wait until morning. I'm sure you're both exhausted after such a long drive. I've put you in one of our cottages, if that's okay? That way, you won't be so cramped up in a double room."

"I didn't realize you had cottages."

The woman smiled, her brown hair pulled up and away from her face. It accented her strange but beautiful greenish-gray eyes. "We are a tourist town, after all. We make room for families and for friends coming down to ski. Our cottages are popular, and the ski lodge gets a lot of our overflow. You are in luck that we still have one unoccupied."

"A cottage would be fantastic until the apartment over the shop can be finished." Hattie looked relieved. She apparently hadn't relished the idea of sharing a double room any more than Cora had.

"They come equipped with kitchens, but you're both welcome to eat with us up here as well. Now, if you'll check in, I'll show you how to get to your cabin once you're done."

The woman was way too chipper for eleven o'clock at night.

"Do you think there's anywhere open where we might get a bite to eat this late?" Hattie handed over her ID and debit card to the front desk clerk.

"I'm sure I can find something for you in the kitchen. We had lasagna for dinner, and there's probably leftovers. I can have Reed bring it down to the cottage for you on his way home. He's just about done in the kitchen anyway."

"That would be appreciated, thank you." Hattie signed some paperwork and collected two keys. "Big Macs just don't taste very good cold."

"You two go get settled in, and I'll have your dinner down soon enough."

"Well, she was nice, wasn't she?" Hattie asked as they reloaded their luggage into the car. She glanced down the path to where they both could see the first of the cottages.

"I don't know if I trust someone that chipper this late."

Hattie laughed. "I was thinking the same thing."

The cabin wasn't large, but it was enough, Cora decided when she threw her luggage on the bed. Her bed seemed to be made out of some kind of pine, and the dresser and chest of drawers matched the bed. The two bedside tables were slightly darker, but not by much. The handmade quilt that covered the bed was gorgeous, though. Cora had a thing for quilts, inherited from her mother.

She pushed thoughts of her mother aside. Two panic attacks in one day was more than she could handle. So she opened her closet and started unpacking. Gran said they'd be here a while, as the upstairs apartment over the shop needed renovating, and as determined as her grandmother was to get the store up and running, Cora guessed the construction crew would start on the store first.

Since tomorrow was Friday, they decided she'd register for school tomorrow, but not start until Monday. The school was fine with it, considering her circumstances. That would give her the weekend to get used to the town and calm herself about starting a new school in the middle of the semester.

Her hand brushed against cool metal, and she yanked it back, not wanting to look at the photo she knew was there. It was of her family, all of them at the beach this last summer. Cora's eyes filled with fresh tears, and she brushed them away.

No.

Slamming the lid of her suitcase closed, she ran from the bedroom and all the pain that photo would pull out of her. With that pain would come guilt, and then the panic would creep back in. Her heartbeat was already more than a little fast, and she sat down on the overly comfortable couch and focused on taking long, deep breaths like the doctor had shown her.

It took her several minutes to beat back the panic, but she did it. No small feat either. Her doctor would say she was getting better, but she would say she was just getting better at hiding everything she felt.

She'd been out partying while her family suffered and ultimately died. She'd never forgive herself. That was a fact everyone refused to understand, even her gran.

"Cora?"

She jumped at the sound of Hattie's voice. "Yeah, Gran?"

"You okay?"

"Not really, but it is what it is."

"I know it's hard, Buggy, but we'll get through it. We're starting over in a new town, and we'll make friends and the loss we suffered will ease a little. I won't lie and say it'll go away, because it doesn't. It just eases enough to let us breathe through the worst of it."

"Right now it hurts too much to draw in a breath," Cora whispered, her voice a little broken.

"I know, honey." Gran sat down and hugged her. "I know."

The doorbell rang. "That's probably our dinner. Why don't you go get it, and I'll see if I can find plates and silverware in the kitchen?"

Nodding, Cora wiped at her eyes and went to answer the door. She was starving. She'd eaten her nuggets hours ago, and her stomach growled, reminding her of that fact.

When she opened the door, her breath caught. Not because the guy standing there was overly cute. He *was* cute, but in an average kind of way. She'd dated guys cuter than him. There was something about him that tugged at her, though, like an itch that couldn't be scratched. He stood taller than her by a good foot, his dark brown hair blending into the hoodie he wore. Green eyes, so bright she wasn't even sure the darkness could hide them, stared back at her.

He was carrying a tray laden with covered plates and a bag bearing the inn's logo.

"Where do you want this?"

His voice was deeper than she expected, more like the man's voice he'd grow into. And she liked it.

He cleared his throat when she didn't answer, and she heard her grandmother laugh from behind her.

"Just bring it in and put it on the table, please." Hattie gently pushed her out of the doorway, and Cora felt her face flame up. She seriously didn't just stand there like some dumbstruck teenager, did she?

Well, she *was* a dumbstruck teenager.

So she gave herself an out.

Reed moved past her, and his smell tickled her nose. He smelled faintly of motor oil and leather. Normally she'd scrunch her nose up, but not this time. It smelled delicious on him.

Her grandmother handed him a ten-dollar bill. "I appreciate you dropping this off to us on your way home . . . Reed, wasn't it?"

"Yes, ma'am." He nodded and took the cash. "Thanks for this too."

"Well, you made me laugh by tongue-tying my granddaughter, so it was well worth it."

His eyes swept over to Cora, and a hint of a smile appeared. "I should get going. Do you ladies need anything else?"

"No, but thank you." Hattie walked him to the door and closed it behind him.

Cora sank down in the first chair and ducked her head. Embarrassed wasn't quite the word for how she was feeling just then.

"Cute little fella, isn't he?"

"That boy is anything but little, Gran."

She wagged her eyebrows at Cora.

"Gross, Gran. Get your head out of the gutter."

"A woman's head should always stay partially in the gutter or she'll have no fun in life."

"Grandma!"

Hattie laughed and sat down on the couch, her white hair on full display. She had it cut in a short, cute style that suited her well. "I have so much to teach you, Bug-a-boo."

Cougar grandmother on the loose. No wonder they only saw her on birthdays and holidays.

The smell of cheese and sauce distracted her from her embarrassment. The lasagna practically bubbled with gooey yumminess. They'd even sent down garlic bread, cold water, and utensils.

Then Cora read the note.

Sorry, all we had left was vegetable lasagna.

She showed it to Gran.

They were both meat lovers.

Gran leaned down and sniffed. "Still smells good. I say we walk on the wild side and ignore the fact it's all veggies."

Cora shrugged and dug in. It tasted good, and her stomach rumbled in agreement. "It's safe."

Hattie sighed and shoved a big heaping bite into her mouth. "This does taste good!"

After a few minutes, Cora decided to broach her grandmother's weird declaration from before.

"Okay, Gran, we're here, we're settled, and we have dinner. It's time to tell me what you meant about us having to run."

Gran took a drink of her water. "I wouldn't say we're settled until all the boxes have been unpacked."

"Gran . . ."

Hattie sighed. "I hoped you'd forgotten about that."

"Not a chance."

"I'd expected to have more time to figure out how to explain things to you."

"Mom always says to just spit it out, even if the truth hurts."

"I wish it were as simple as that." Hattie stood and went down the hall toward her bedroom. Cora stared after her, bewildered.

She was acting strange, even for her grandmother. Her dad always called his mother a free-range chicken. She roamed free and never lived her life with regrets. Flighty was her mother's term for Hattie.

But what if there had been threats made against her and Cora? What if the accident that took her family from her wasn't really an accident? The police might have told her gran something they thought she couldn't handle. After having to make the decisions that night and her family dying . . . she'd been a mess. They may have confided in her grandmother.

Hopefully, she was about to find out.

CHAPTER 4

*W*hen Hattie came back, she was carrying a small wooden box.

"Do you remember when you were a little girl and you snuck into your father's workshop?"

"Yes. I thought he was going to have a heart attack, he yelled so loud." She'd been seven and only curious as to what kind of toy her father was making. They didn't just own a toy store. Her family were toy makers, hand-carved toys being their specialty. She'd picked up a piece of white wood, and her father walked in at the same time. It hadn't been pretty, and he'd kept his workshop locked after that.

"He had good reason." Hattie handed her the box. "Does this look familiar?"

Cora took the small box, no bigger than the palm of her hand. It was carved with delicate yet intricate designs. The wood was smooth and white. It wasn't painted white; that was the natural color of the wood. She tried to find a latch to open it, but there was none. There was no seam at all to indicate where it opened.

"Is it a jewelry box or something?"

"Or something," Hattie muttered. "That box is the reason our family died."

Cora dropped it faster than a hot french fry fresh from the deep fryer. That little box was the reason for the accident?

"What do you mean, Gran?"

"They weren't in a simple accident."

"I knew it!" All of her fears from earlier came rushing back. The police must have told Hattie something they didn't think she could handle. "What did the police say? Did someone make threats?"

"This has nothing to do with the police, Cora, but our family history." Hattie reached down and picked up the box from where it had fallen, cradling it gently.

"I don't understand."

"I know you don't. You were never meant to know any of this, but you are the last of your father's children."

"You're not making sense, Gran. Did the police tell you someone caused the accident on purpose?"

Hattie shook her head. "No, Bug-a-boo. This box told me."

"How can a box tell you?"

"Inside of this box is a fire demon."

What the . . . "Gran, what the hell?"

"Language, young lady." For the first time in a long time, Hattie looked her age. Her body hunched in on itself. "Our family, specifically those with Hartwood blood, have been designing demon traps since before the Roman empire."

"Demon traps?" There was no hiding the derision in Cora's voice. Her gran was off her freaking rocker. Demons? Seriously?

"This is why I wanted more time to explain it to you." Hattie sighed and ran a hand through her pixie-cut hair. "I didn't believe it either when your grandfather told me."

"Grandpa believed in all this nonsense?" Cora whispered.

"The Hartwood men usually only share this secret with the male members of the family. The women are kept out of it."

"That's stupid." Not that Cora believed this nonsense, but she disagreed with that archaic way of thinking. A woman could do anything a man could do. Mostly, anyway.

"Your grandfather agreed. It's why he told me. Did you know you're the first girl born into the Hartwood family since 1742?"

"That can't be right."

"It's true. It's why your grandfather was fighting so hard for your father to tell you about the boxes. He thought it was a sign, you being born under a solstice moon."

"Isn't that witch stuff? Mom and Dad were Christians."

"Not witch stuff, pagan stuff," Hattie clarified. "The practice goes back to the very old world, when Christianity was just beginning to be whispered about. It was the Christians who began to worship differently and then branded everyone else pagans. Did you know that?"

Cora shook her head, confused. What did this have to do with anything?

"Our family worshiped the old gods for a very long time before we converted to Christianity, and we learned how to create the boxes to trap demons and other harmful spirits from those days. I just wanted you to understand how we learned to do this, or rather how the Hartwoods learned to do it."

"Gran, I . . . why are you saying all this? Losing Mom and Dad and Billy . . . it hurt. I hurt all the time. Why would you make it worse by telling me some kind of scary fairy tale?"

Tears shimmered in Hattie's eyes. "I'm telling you because you need to know, Cora. You need to be on constant alert for the woman who caused the accident."

"How do you know it wasn't an accident? Dad lost control of the car and flipped it, going over the hill. It's awful, but there's nothing nefarious going on."

Cora's hands started to shake as she talked about that night. She could feel the panic starting to claw its way up her throat as she imagined them spinning out of control and falling down the ravine when the car went off the road. What did they feel? Were they in pain? Did her mom scream and try to reach her brother? Did her dad know it was useless?

"Cora!" Her gran snapped her fingers in front of Cora's face, bringing her out of her thoughts, but the panic remained. Hattie got up and came back with one of her anxiety pills. She took it gratefully and allowed her grandmother to help her with the water bottle. Her hands were shaking that badly.

"I'm going to find you a therapist first thing tomorrow morning. Saundra should know someone." Hattie proceeded to rub Cora's back until some of the panic subsided. "There, you're feeling better already."

"I'm sorry," Cora said miserably. "I don't know why this keeps happening."

"Because you've suffered a traumatic loss, sweetheart. Your mind and your body have to heal from that. None of this is your fault."

"You need to stop with all this nonsense, Gran. It's not good for me."

"I wish I could, but I can't. I had to get us somewhere safe, somewhere we couldn't be found."

"Gran . . ." Cora took a shaky breath.

"No, you have to listen to me, Cora Jean. I received a phone call from the woman whose lover is trapped in that box. She wants him back and said if I didn't let him out, she'd do to you what she did to the others."

"What?" *No. No. No.* This couldn't be happening.

"I can't open that box, Cora. I'm not a Hartwood by birth. Only a Hartwood can open it. It's what makes our traps so useful. They're immune to magic. Once a spirit or demon is trapped in them, they're there for life unless a Hartwood lets them out."

"You're serious." For the first time since this conversation began, she actually looked at her grandmother. The woman was as serious as a heart attack. Her eyes, which usually always laughed, were somber and full of nothing but honesty.

"I am. As soon as the call ended, I called an old friend of mine, Saundra Beaumont. She's the head of the Luna Coven here in Havenwood Falls. It's because of her we have a safe place.

Havenwood Falls has protections in place that will hide us. If the witch follows us, she'll trigger an alarm that will set a manhunt in motion for her. She can't get to you here."

"Coven . . ." Cora whispered, her mind reeling.

"It's a lot to take in, Buggy, I know, but I'm telling you the truth."

"Then why not let me try to open the box? Give her what she wants?"

"Because your father told me the creature in that box is one of the most dangerous demons he's ever come across. He devours whole families in fire. Letting him go free would be condemning who knows how many innocents. No. Your father died to protect people. I won't let that be in vain."

"I'm not saying I believe you, Gran, but I don't want anyone else to get hurt either." The anxiety medicine was finally starting to really work, and a calmness came over her. She relished the feeling, because she hadn't been truly calm without meds since that night.

"I have all your grandfather's journals. He thought one day you might need to know how to build the traps, and he knew your father would never tell you."

"So Grampa was a forward-thinking man of the times?"

Hattie laughed. "Your grandfather truly believed in women's rights. He thought we deserved the same opportunities as men and did a little lobbying in his day for equal pay. And when it comes to the family secret, he firmly believed you should be told and taught how to make the traps. Your birth was a sign to him."

Cora wasn't sure what to think. Her grandmother wouldn't lie to her, of that she was sure. She was a jokester, but not about something as serious as the death of her only son. How she was supposed to believe all this, now that was another story altogether. With the anxiety meds in her system, she wasn't freaking out, though, and it allowed her to see how serious her grandmother was. She believed every word she was saying, and Cora had to decide if she should believe it too.

But how could she not? If what her grandmother said was true, then every single thing she'd ever believed was gone. If demons and ghosts were real, what else was real? She ate while she thought, letting the warm delicious gooey cheese help to soothe her. Food had always been her place of comfort.

And for the super high metabolism she'd always had, she was grateful. She'd hate to give up her favorite things when stressing.

"Gran, did you ever see one of the things Grampa trapped in those boxes?"

"I did, Cora. That's why I believe what I'm telling you. I witnessed it firsthand."

Well, how was she supposed to argue with that?

"You said we'd be safe here, that there were protections in place? What's to stop this witch from just coming back?"

Hattie smiled. "There's a memory spell in place. Once you enter Havenwood Falls and then leave, you lose all memory of the Falls and the people here."

"So if I go away to college, I'll forget you?" Alarm splintered her calm, and she sat her plate down for fear of dropping it. "You're all I have, Gran. I don't want to lose my memories of you."

And it sounded even to her like she was beginning to believe the nonsense.

"You won't completely forget me, only our time here in Havenwood Falls. You can still call me and send me emails and texts. Don't panic, Buggy. There are online classes if you don't want to go away, and even if you do leave, when it's finally safe for you to leave, I'll always pull you back. You're not going to lose me, Cora."

"You can't promise that, Gran. No one can."

"You're right." Hattie got up and came to sit beside her, pulling her into a hug. "Our days on this earth aren't guaranteed, but what I will promise is that I'll be here fighting with the Grim Reaper for every single day, for you. I'm not going anywhere for a good long time."

"You swear?"

"I pinkie swear." She hooked her pinkie with Cora's and winked. "Now, let's finish our dinner and get some sleep. Tomorrow is going to be a long day."

Cora nodded and did as she was bid. Her mind was in shock, and when she went to bed, for once she fell into a dreamless sleep.

CHAPTER 5

*M*orning brought with it a whole world of new anxieties for Cora. Not only was she dealing with her guilt about the accident, but now she added a new fear to the mix. Someone was trying to kill her over a demon trapped in a box only she could open.

She wasn't sure she quite believed it, but she knew her gran wasn't lying. Hattie might be a flake and quirky, but she loved Cora with everything she had. Cora could feel it every time she was in the same room with Hattie.

She took a shower and then rummaged around in the kitchen for coffee. There was a coffee maker, but no coffee. She really needed caffeine this morning.

"Gran!"

"What?" came her grandmother's answering shout.

"Is there a place to get coffee around here?"

"I'm sure there is." Gran stuck her head out of her bedroom, the wet strands of hair sticking to her skin. "Why don't you take the car and look for some?"

"Thanks. I need me some java."

"You and me both. Just be careful."

Careful was something she'd be from now on. Driving gave her hives, but she knew it was necessary, and so she faced that fear every time she got behind the wheel. She needed to get from point A to point B, and driving was the fastest way.

Once she was on her way, she looked around at the square. Several shops stood out to her, specifically Coffee Haven. Truthfully, she could have walked, it was so close, but she was freezing. For a beach girl, the weather here was not a check in the pro column. It was too cold to walk.

For her at least. People were out everywhere in light jackets as they strolled through the square and along Main Street. Everyone seemed happy and at ease, the way she was just a few weeks ago. Shaking her head before she slipped back into that dark place, she parked and hurried into the cafe.

The place was light and airy with all sorts of artwork on the walls. Cora fell in love with it, and all dark thoughts of no Starbucks in town went right out of her head as the scents of fresh coffee and pastries invaded her nostrils. *Starbucks who?*

She got in line and studied the menu as she shuffled forward. They had everything she loved and then things she'd never heard of. This was not a morning to be adventurous, so she ordered a caramel latte and a large coffee with hazelnut syrup for her gran. She also bought two large pastries. Breakfast of champions.

Thanking the woman at the counter, she turned and ran right into someone, spilling her coffee all over them.

"Oh, my gosh, I'm so sorry!"

She looked right up into a pair of green eyes, the same eyes she'd looked into last night. While they weren't amused, they weren't angry either.

He shook his head and looked down at his jacket, now covered in coffee stains.

"Reed, are you okay?" A girl about their age rushed over to him and gave Cora the side eye that said *who are you and get the f out right now.*

"I'm fine, Josie." His voice was just as deep as it was last night, and it still made her shiver. He wasn't built, but he wasn't small either. Nice and normal, Emily would call him, but sometimes nice and normal was better than built like a linebacker. At least it was for Reed.

"You need to watch where you're going." Josie glared at Cora from where she was hanging onto Reed's arm. Girlfriend?

"I'm sorry. I turned around and wasn't expecting anyone to be right there." He had been awfully close.

"She's right. I saw her turning and should have stepped back. This is my fault, not hers."

Josie made this clucking noise, but the back-off signs shooting like stars out of her eyes said she didn't think it was all his fault.

"Let me rebuy your coffees for you." Reed gently disentangled himself from Josie and turned those very serious eyes of his right on Cora. She felt like squirming under their direct stare.

"Oh, no, please. I dumped it all over you. The least you can let me do is buy yours for you."

He smiled and dimples appeared. Oh dear God, the boy had dimples!

"Sure. Cora, right?"

She nodded, suddenly tongue-tied.

"I'm Reed, but you know that, and this is my friend Josie."

It wasn't lost on me or Josie that he introduced her as his "friend."

"Hi. It's nice to meet you both." Not. She'd rather Josie walk away. She wasn't up for all that anger this morning. She was finally starting to feel less like a zombie, and she wanted to stay Zen. Waiting on her morning dose of caffeine was starting to eat into her Zen-ness. "What kind of coffee did you want?"

"Just a large regular coffee."

Cora nodded and placed her order again. Thankfully, the pastries survived.

"So, are you heading over to school?" Reed asked as they moved aside to wait for the order.

"No. My Gran and I are going over later today so I can register, but I'm not starting until next week."

"Lucky," Reed drawled, his dimples coming back out to play.

Sweet baby Jesus, please don't let me say something stupid right now or get tongue-tied.

"You're not a tourist?" Josie looked a little green around the edges.

Cora shook her head. "Not a tourist. My gran and I are moving in."

"You're the one opening the new toy store, right?"

"Yeah," Cora answered Reed. "It's been in my family for over two hundred years. We do a lot of handcrafted toys as well as the mainstream ones."

"Like those lame wooden toys that are ancient?" Josie's tone was as derisive as the look on her face.

"My dad took a lot of pride in his work, and those lame wooden toys are the ones most parents want their kids to have when they're young because they're not a hazard to them like all that plastic junk. People contacted my dad daily to commission toys, one-of-a-kind toys that you'll not find in any department store. So keep your snotty little attitude to yourself, especially when you don't know what you're talking about."

Josie's eyes went wide and before she could say anything, the girl behind the counter told them their drinks were ready. Cora took hers, gave Reed a nod, and hurried out the door, anger burning in every fiber of her being. That nasty girl had better learn to keep her mouth shut.

Tears pricked Cora's eyes as she got into the car. She'd overreacted, she knew, but the pain of losing her father was so fresh, anger was easier to deal with and didn't bring on the panic attacks.

The knock on the car window startled her, and she did this meow-like scream. She let out a shaky breath when she saw it was Reed. Rolling down the window, she arched a brow.

"Hey, I'm sorry about Josie."

"Not your fault she's a grade A bi—"

"She is," Reed cut her off. "She's also a good friend who wants to be more than friends, but I've told her again and again I don't want that. She can get possessive, and that's what that was in there. I told her to leave you alone."

"I can defend myself," Cora said, feeling a little raw. Her emotions were running high, and if she didn't get away from everything, she might have another panic attack. She hadn't even brought her meds, because she was just going a short distance from the cottage.

"I know you can." Reed gave her a little smile. "I have to work tonight, but I'm free tomorrow. Why don't you let me show you around town?"

"I . . . I don't know. We just got here and . . ." She was rambling. Bad habit of hers when she got super nervous. "I'm dealing with some stuff . . ."

"It's cool," Reed said. "I'll catch you at school or maybe I'll see you up at the inn." He gave her one last smile and turned and walked away.

Cora let out a breath she didn't realize she'd been holding and let her head drop to the steering wheel. She was such a dork.

Not that spending a whole day with Reed would have been a hardship, but with her anxiety like it was, she'd been afraid of freaking out. And it didn't seem right she should be out there having fun when her family had been buried just a few weeks ago.

Sighing, she started the car and headed back to the cottage. At least within those four walls she didn't have to deal with anything but missing her family.

CHAPTER 6

*R*egistering for school hadn't taken nearly as long as Cora thought it would, but then again, she'd never moved before. Her family had been in the same house since she was three. Her grandmother filled out all the paperwork while she sat and did a whole lot of nothing.

The thought of starting a new school in the middle of the semester was harrowing. Everyone already had their own little cliques, and finding one where she'd fit in was going to be next to impossible. She'd seen it happen at her own school. Cora liked to think she'd never been the mean girl to a new student. She always tried to say hello and make people feel welcome, but who knew if there was someone like that at Havenwood Falls High?

She pushed those thoughts aside as they pulled up to the building that would house the new toy store. It didn't look too bad, on the outside at least. It could use a coat of paint, but even that wasn't bad. Her grandmother said it was a double-wide building, which could house both the toy store and her sugar shop if she wanted to do it. She loved making candy of all kinds, but since her family died, she hadn't been in the mood.

"What about the workshop?" She pulled the sides of her brand new coat together as she waited for Hattie to unlock the building.

They'd just come from the agent's office and signed the paperwork for the shop. The key looked to be sticking in the lock when her gran tried it.

"The basement?" Hattie gave up and handed the key to Cora. "Here, you try."

Cora stuck the key in the lock and jiggled it several times until it finally turned. "We need to call a locksmith and get the locks changed anyway. Do you know if they have a security company in town?"

"I'm sure they do. I'm having lunch with Saundra in a little bit, and I'll ask her then. Do you want to come, Buggy?"

"No, I think I'll stay here and clean up a little, then take all our shopping bags back to the cottage." She pushed the door open and gasped. The windows were covered so you couldn't see inside, and now she understood why. The place was covered in dirt and abandoned furniture. "No wonder it's so cheap. It's going to cost thousands just for garbage removal."

Hattie sighed. "This is not what I was hoping for. God knows what it looks like upstairs."

Both women grimaced and picked their way through the garbage to a door toward the back. Two empty rooms and a staircase lay hidden behind it. Both rooms were just as dirty as the front room, and Cora took the stairs first. They looked shaky, and she'd rather break a leg herself than let her grandmother be injured. Who knew how well she'd heal at her age?

There was another door at the top of the stairs, but she didn't need to worry about a lock. The door was hanging off its hinges. It took her minute to get it pushed aside so they could enter. The room was small and closed off, the carpet ruined and wallpaper peeling. The room overlooked the back parking lot, hidden from the square. The window was pushed up, and she saw dark spots underneath it. Who knew how long rain and snow had been getting in?

"I think they're gonna have to start with this floor first, Gran. There's water damage."

"Hell's bells," her grandmother muttered, and Cora suppressed a grin. Her gran was no stranger to four-letter words, but she tried to tone it down around her grandkids. Not that it worked out well, but she did try.

"We may be at the inn longer than expected. Maybe we should see if the apartment complex leases by the month." Hattie started to explore and moved through the doorway. "Kitchen's in here. You don't want to look at it."

Cora laughed and moved off down the small hallway. The first two doors were bedrooms, and the last door was a fairly spacious bathroom. It stank, and as soon as her eyes landed on the toilet, she covered her nose and backed out.

"Gran, don't go in the bathroom."

"Why?"

"Uh, it's painted brown."

"Why would anyone paint a wall brown for any reason?" Hattie curled her nose and did just what Cora told her not to. She let out a squeal and ran, nearly knocking Cora over in the process.

"I told you not to go in there."

"You should have said someone smeared crap on the walls."

"I did. I said they painted the walls brown. It was a nicer way of saying it."

Hattie glared. "There is no nice way of saying that!" She pointed toward the offending room.

Cora shrugged, suppressing a smile. Her grandmother was the only person who'd been able to make her smile since that awful night at the hospital, and for that she was grateful. Her mom always said laughter made everything better, and Cora had to admit, when she laughed, some of the ache inside her eased up just a little.

"Why don't you take the car to lunch, then swing by here and pick me up afterward?" Cora asked. "We'll find the grocery store and stock up on a few things."

"Sounds like a plan, but I'm not sure you'll be able to do much here without cleaning supplies."

"True. I hadn't thought about that." She shrugged.

"I think I'll walk around and get the lay of the land. I can even walk back to the inn from here. The exercise will do me good."

"Are you sure?" Her grandmother hated leaving her alone. She'd seen firsthand just how broken Cora was, and leaving her to wallow in grief by herself wasn't high on Hattie's to-do list.

"Yeah, I'll be fine. I might even swing back by the coffee place and get some more of those blueberry scones you oohed and ahhed over this morning."

"You know I can never say no to sugar." Her grandmother winked. "Of any kind."

"Gross, Gran!"

Hattie laughed. She loved shocking her granddaughter.

"We'll get you feeling up to enjoying some sugar of your own, maybe in the form of that little hottie who showed up at our doorstep last night." Hattie wagged her eyebrows suggestively.

"Gran!" Cora gasped, pretending to be outraged. Truthfully, she was rolling inside with laughter.

"What? Someone has to get you back in the saddle. Besides, I hear this town is known for its festivals. Did you not notice all the harvest-themed decorations that are up everywhere? There are even some shops that already have Christmas lights up. We'll get you a date in no time . . ."

"Gran, I'm not up to festivals and all that other stuff just yet. I don't even know if I want to do Thanksgiving this year." Just like that, all her happiness got sucked away.

It wasn't fair that she got to go on living while her family were all cold and buried beneath the dirt.

Hattie came over and hugged her tight. "I'm sorry, Buggy. I'm just trying to take your mind off things."

"I know, and I appreciate it, but doing all that and pretending to be happy?" Cora shook her head. "It feels like I can't breathe most days, Gran. Going out and having fun at a festival is so far from what I'm up for, it's not even funny."

"It's okay, baby girl. We'll take this as slow as you need to, and if you don't want to do Thanksgiving, that's fine with me.

Less for me to have to do while trying to get the store ready to open."

"Uh, Gran, I don't think this place is going to be ready by Black Friday, especially if they have to replace sub-flooring up here, and I hate to ask what the electrical and plumbing looks like."

"When did you get to be so construction-y?"

"When I started watching HGTV while I did my homework."

"Then maybe you should supervise repairs, and we'll save some money."

Cora scrunched up her nose. "I'm not that good, Gran. Besides, if I did that, then you wouldn't get to ogle all the guys coming in and out on work crews."

"See, you're starting to get to know your grandmother all too well. You're even looking out for my fantasy daydream material."

"Ewwwww."

Hattie laughed and hugged Cora. "You know I love you, don't you?"

"I do, Gran, and I love you."

"Well, now that we've got all the mushy stuff out of the way, let's go back downstairs and try to start making plans for the store until it's time for me to meet Saundra."

Cora nodded and followed her grandmother back downstairs.

CHAPTER 7

*C*ora stepped outside and zipped up her new fur-lined coat. The light pink color matched her hair perfectly. New boots kept her feet warm as she walked down the path leading to Main Street. She'd changed her mind about walking around town earlier and asked her gran to take her back to the cottage before her lunch with Saundra. She'd warned Cora she wanted to meet with the contractors after lunch and would be gone a while. Cora found herself alone with her thoughts far longer than she'd expected. Not a good place for her to be.

So she decided to take the walk she'd put off earlier and get to know her new town. This morning had introduced her to the new store, and her curiosity got the best of her as the day wore on. She wanted to do a little exploring before the sun went down.

Hattie assured her they were safe here, that the person responsible for her family's death couldn't reach her here. Cora wasn't so sure. If everything her grandmother said was true, then she wasn't going to bet on her safety behind some kind of magical ward. She'd taken the small pocket knife her father gave her on her tenth birthday and slipped it into her jacket pocket just in case. Normally she used it for carving, but it would work as a weapon too.

She would give her gran one thing—Havenwood Falls was

breathtaking with the Colorado mountains as a backdrop. The town was nestled right up against a mountain range, giving it an almost storybook quality. She strolled along Main Street, looking at the shops, then wandered to the fountain in the middle of the square.

"Hey."

Cora couldn't help the scream that escaped her at the sound of that voice. She turned to see Reed standing there, wearing jeans and a light jacket.

He held up his hands. "Easy. It's just me, your friendly neighborhood boy next door."

She let out a shaky sigh that turned into something resembling a laugh. "Sorry. I . . . I'm a little jumpy."

"You okay?"

She nodded. "New place, you know?"

He studied her, and she could tell he didn't believe her, but he didn't push either.

"I saw you standing here on my way to work and thought I'd say hi. You looked a little lonely."

She didn't quite know what to say to that. The truth was she *had* felt lonely. She needed a better poker face.

"My gran is out, and I guess I got a case of cabin fever."

He nodded. "Come on up to the inn, and I'll see if I can filch you some sweets. Michaela makes the best desserts this side of the mountain. Since I'm working in the kitchen today, I should be able to swipe you some."

"I do have a sweet tooth."

He grinned. "I guessed that this morning, and all that pink and purple hair of yours is another clue."

"Is that so?" Cora asked as she fell into step beside him.

He nodded wisely. "Yup. My mom says anyone who dyes their hair to look like candy has a definite weak spot for the sweet stuff."

"Candy?" She self-consciously stroked her hair.

"I'm not dissing your hair. It's cute."

"Yeah?" A warm feeling seeped into her limbs, and she felt a light flush heat her cheeks.

"Yeah. Did you get registered at school okay?"

"It was easier than I thought it would be."

They turned the corner, heading for the inn. "About earlier, I wasn't hitting on you or anything. I was just offering to show you around, maybe get your mind off everything."

Cora went still and turned to look at him. "What do you mean?"

He flushed. "It's just . . . we all know what happened, why you're here. Small town and all that. I was trying to help."

Everyone knew she'd lost her family? It's not like it was a secret or anything, but the thought of everyone knowing . . .

"Not everyone. I know because I work at the inn, and there are gossipmongers in the kitchen. Josie didn't know. If she had, she wouldn't have been so . . ."

"Territorial?"

He shrugged. "I've told her all she and I will ever be is friends. If she doesn't get it through her head, she and I are going to have to stop hanging out for a while. I don't want to hurt her."

Reed gestured toward the inn, and Cora started walking again. She wasn't sure she liked everyone knowing her business, but it made sense they'd know. It really was a small town.

"I hate walking into a room and seeing that pitying look on people's faces." She stopped on the porch and stared out at the town square. "It's part of why I agreed to come here so quickly. No one would know unless I told them. I wouldn't see that look anymore."

"I'm sorry." Reed took her hand and squeezed it. "I was just trying to help."

Cora nodded. She believed him.

"Come on, let's get you all sugared up."

She really didn't want to go inside now, but she put one foot in front of the other and followed him. Reed was just being nice, even if he had made her feel self-conscious. He didn't deserve her anger. As her daddy always said, *suck it up, buttercup, and get it done.*

The inn was bustling today with people downstairs sipping coffee and reading what she assumed were the remnants of this morning's newspaper. The staff seemed to be just there out of the corner of your eye, ready to help before you even realized you needed help.

Her mom would have loved this place. It was so comfortable. As she gazed around, she decided that was the right term for the front area. It was designed so guests would feel more at home.

"It seems busy," Cora noted.

"It's our busy time of the year. The ski slopes are opening, so we get an influx of tourists. It's why I have a job here. I help out in the kitchen when they need me, and I do some maintenance work too."

"Jack of all trades, huh?"

He nodded and put his finger to his lips before hustling her toward the back of the inn, where she assumed the kitchen was. Sure enough, the scent of what she thought was roast chicken tickled her nose. Reed had her wait outside, and she peeked in when he went through the door.

A small kitchen greeted her. There were a few people doing prep work. It looked clean too. That was always a plus. She'd waitressed at a restaurant in Charleston that didn't put too much effort into cleaning. She lasted about a week. She started working at her family's toy shop after that fiasco.

She saw one of the waitstaff coming toward the door and moved out of the way. It would be just her luck to get a black eye or busted nose right before she started a new school due to her own carelessness.

Reed came out a few minutes later, carrying a plate with a huge piece of strawberry shortcake piled high with whipped cream. Her taste buds started to tingle right as her stomach growled.

"Somebody's hungry." Reed handed her the plate and the fork he'd filched.

"I haven't eaten since breakfast."

"In that case, maybe we should wait on the cake and let you eat something first."

He reached for it, and she fake stabbed at him with the fork.

"Don't you dare. I'm starved. Trust me, I eat dessert before dinner all the time."

"Come on, Shortcake. Let's get you settled while I clock in."

She scrunched her nose up at the nickname, which only caused Reed to smirk. He laughed under his breath and led her to a quiet corner in the parlor. Several people glanced her way, but soon turned their attention back to whatever they were doing.

Reed told her he'd be back to check on her. Once he disappeared, she dived into the heavenly dessert. Strawberry shortcake was her favorite . . . outside of the raspberry chocolate deluxe her gran made for her every time she came to visit.

Cora finished her cake and set the plate on the small table beside the armchair she was sitting in. Her gaze wandered back to the people around her. She couldn't help but wonder if any of them were supernatural. Ever since her gran told her about the box, her mind wandered back to all those paranormal romances her mother loved, where the super sexy alpha swooped in and saved the day.

She could use someone to save the day. After everything that had happened, the thought of even more coming at her and her grandmother was debilitating. Cora had been outside feeling alone and scared. She'd give almost anything to have those feelings go away. She didn't want to feel like a victim. Her parents had taught her to never be a victim, to be a survivor, but that's exactly what she felt like right now. Someone who had no control over anything that happened to her. Someone who didn't know how to survive in her new reality.

"Hey."

Reed startled her again. Man, he moved super stealthily. Maybe he was a supernatural creature?

He squatted in front of her, bringing him to eye level with her. His green eyes were bright and open. "You doing okay?"

"Yeah, just people-watching. Thanks for bringing me here. I needed to be around people."

"That's what we do here in Havenwood Falls." He flashed her a smile. "We take care of each other, and you're part of our community now. Plus, anyone with hair like yours shouldn't be sad all the time. If I can help you to feel better, I will."

That was the nicest thing anyone had said to her in a long, long time. It caused the butterflies to flutter to life in her stomach again, and her mouth got all dry. Nervous. He made her nervous, but a good nervous. The kind of nervous her mom said she'd feel one day when she met the right person.

"I, uh . . ."

He winked. "If you're up for seeing the town, my offer still stands. I'll show you around tomorrow. It could be fun, and I know fun's probably the last thing you're up for, but I promise it's the only thing that's going to help you heal."

"You sound like you know something about that."

"I do. My brother died a few years ago. Took me a while to get myself out of a dark hole. Still hurts every day, but some days are easier than others. Like today. All that rainbow hair of yours distracted me from a little pain."

Cora didn't know what to say. Again.

"Don't answer me now." He took her hand and wrote a number in her palm. "Call me tomorrow if you want a tour guide."

She looked at the number in her hand. People didn't do that anymore. They traded numbers through their cells. It was old school, but it was charming.

"Thank you."

He tweaked her nose. "I have to get to the kitchen, but stick around for dinner if you want. Our roast chicken is pretty famous."

"I made plans with Gran already."

His half smile curled her toes.

"Then I'll see you tomorrow."

"I didn't say I was gonna call."

"You will." He jumped up and leaned down to kiss the top of her head. "You will, Shortcake."

Then he strolled off and left her staring after him, confused and guilty for feeling the butterflies.

Who the heck was he?

CHAPTER 8

"Why are we here at six in the morning, Gran?"

Cora yawned and stared at the empty streets of the town square. The heavy clouds overhead hinted at bad weather. She pulled her coat tighter around her and tugged the key out of her grandmother's hands. The locksmith needed to get here today.

"Because we agreed to meet the contractor at six-thirty. If we agree on his bid, he can start work by eight."

"You mean *you* agreed to meet him here. I still don't know why you dragged me out of a perfectly comfortable, *warm* bed."

The key turned, and Cora opened the door. "That's why I dragged you out here. I'd be standing here in the cold until he arrived because that cursed key hates me."

"Did you contact the locksmith yesterday?"

"No, I forgot. Saundra and I talked for a long time yesterday, and it slipped my mind. I did, however, remember to have them turn on the electricity." Hattie flipped the light switch, and one single bulb in the light fixture flickered to life.

"Uh-huh," Cora muttered and walked over to where she'd seen a thermostat yesterday. She set it to heat, and then a loud clanging noise started up. That nasty heat smell filtered through the vents. "At least we can stay warm."

A louder noise followed that statement, and then the noise from the heat pump died.

"You had to say it, didn't you?" Hattie shook her head.

There was a knock on the open door behind them, and a man stepped in carrying a clipboard, a toolbelt wrapped around his waist. He was an older man, maybe a little older than her father had been, but he was quite fit in his jean jacket, red flannel shirt, and well-worn jeans. His hair was a light brown, but a few strands of silver were starting to show at his temples. She couldn't help but notice his right earlobe was missing, too. How in the world—she looked away to keep from staring. He moved with a grace Cora would never have. If this man wasn't some kind of supernatural creature, then she might as well stop guessing.

"Mrs. Hartwood?"

"Yes, I'm Hattie, and this is my granddaughter, Cora. You're Mike McCabe?"

"Yes, ma'am. Everyone calls me Big Mike, though." He shook her hand. "Owner of McCabe & Sons Construction. Saundra Beaumont said you had an urgent job?"

"We do. We want to have the shop up and running by Black Friday. The apartment upstairs needs to be redone too."

"The toy shop?"

"How did you know we were opening a toy shop?" Cora asked.

His blue eyes cut to her, and she glanced away. There was something there in his eyes that was very commanding, something that made her feel the need to respect him. His eyes were stern, like her grandfather's used to be. Maybe that's why she felt the need to respect him.

"It's a small town. Everyone knows everything."

Cora sighed.

"It's not a bad thing. It means help is always just a shout away, should you need it."

That brought her eyes back up to his. Did he know about the threats to her?

She had a feeling he did.

"If you give me a few minutes, I'll walk the property and give you a list of what I think you're going to need."

"Will it be a problem to add in a workshop downstairs and make sure the outside resembles the old shop? The design has been in our family for hundreds of years."

"It won't be a problem. We're big on tradition here. If we need to, there's a very good architect in town who can help us create what you're looking for. You have pictures?"

"We have a website," Cora told him. "It has pictures of the shop. Also, we want one section of the main floor to house a candy shop and a kitchen somewhere as well."

He frowned. "We have a sweet shop . . ."

"We're not looking to take away any tourist or local business from existing shops in town," Hattie hurried to assure him. "Cora makes homemade candy like fudge and caramels and hand-spun lollipops. We'd probably bring in candy for a section for kids to build their own bags of candy too."

Mike nodded, his eyes giving nothing away in his weathered face. He looked like someone who spent a lot of time outside, but then again, he was in construction. Made sense for him to be so tan and rugged.

"This is going to take me a while to walk through, and I need to contact that architect I told you about. I can have him here in about an hour to go over everything you want to do. Why don't you two go grab breakfast, and I'll text you when we're ready to talk about the job?"

"That sounds good." Hattie nodded. "Where's the best place to get breakfast?"

"Let's just walk to Coffee Haven. That's where I got the scones from yesterday."

"You know I can't turn down pastries."

The two of them wandered over to the coffee shop and ordered pastries and coffees. Once they were seated, Hattie leaned down and just inhaled the scent of her warm scone. She bypassed her coffee for a huge bite of the blueberry sweet.

"So, Gran, do you think we can get the store open by Black Friday?" Cora sipped her coffee, relishing the taste. She loved coffee more than she did most food, outside of sweets. "I know we talked about this already, but is it even worth it? I know it's a touristy town, but most people are home for Thanksgiving, aren't they? Our online sale should be more than enough."

"There are lots of families here in Havenwood Falls that shop for their kids just the same as everyone else. With a toy store right here in town, we should be able to do very well, because they won't have to travel to the big box stores and deal with the crowds. This is also the beginning of the ski season, and there should be lots of tourists in town, or so I've been told. I take it you've decided to do the candy store?"

"I thought about what you said, about needing something to take your mind off everything, and I guess I need something too."

"That's good, honey. That's very good." Hattie smiled at her. "I did find a therapist right here in town I think you should see. It'll be good for you."

"I don't know, Gran . . ." What if people in her new school found out she was seeing a shrink? Not only would she be the new girl who lost her entire family, but one who needed a shrink too.

"This is something I'm going to put my foot down on, Cora. You need to talk to someone."

Gran hardly ever called her anything but Bug or Bug-a-boo. She was serious when she used her name.

"Fine."

"Good girl. Do you know what you want the candy section of the store to look like?"

"Have you ever seen Sweet Pete's? It was featured on that show *The Profit*. He has all these bright colors, and I was thinking that maybe we could update the store itself with some brighter colors to match the candy store."

"I guess maybe we should update it, since we're starting over from scratch. We haven't had a redesign since the seventies."

"Trust me, I know."

Hattie laughed. "If we do the redesign, we might not be open for Black Friday."

"It doesn't matter to me. We can advertise a big Black Friday sale online."

"When did you get so business savvy?"

"I've been working in the store since I was little in one way or another, Gran. Daddy taught me how to do the books and the day-to-day because I really liked it. I learned the online business and how to market from Mom. She was the techie person. She showed me everything about it, from the back office to how to create and send out our newsletter full of sales."

"I had no idea you were so involved with the store. I just assumed your father would have turned the business over to your brother, all things considered. It's how it's done in our family."

"That's archaic and not at all fair." Cora didn't like the thought of getting shut out of the business one day by her father. He seemed so happy she loved working there. She just assumed she and her brother would inherit the store together once her father decided to retire or he passed.

"No, Buggy, it's not fair. But it's just us now, and we have the chance to change all that."

A sliver of pain knifed across her chest. She knew she wasn't alone. She had her Gran, but she wanted her mommy and daddy and her little brother back. That was what wasn't fair. She'd give anything to have them back.

"Bug, you okay?"

"Yeah, I'm fine. Just tired. Someone woke me up before the crack of dawn."

Maybe going to see this therapist would help. She hated talking to her gran about how sad she was. It only upset the woman and there was nothing she could do to help Cora that she wasn't already doing.

Gran finished her pastry. "I'm going to be at the store most of the day. Do you have any plans or do you want to come hang out with your super cool and hip grandma?"

Super cool she might be, but she could be super weird too and very cougarish when it came to men. She flirted more than Cora.

"Well, I uh . . ."

"You uh what?" Gran's eyes sharpened, and Cora felt like squirming.

"Reed asked me again if I wanted him to show me around town today."

"The hottie from the inn?"

"Gran, that sounds so wrong coming out of your mouth."

"I may be old, but I'm not dead. Are you going?"

"I don't know. What if I'm out and I have a panic attack?" That fear had bothered her all night. Her panic attacks were severe when they happened. No one wanted a guy to see them all messed up like that. She'd never be able to look at Reed again.

"But what if you don't?"

"I don't know," Cora said miserably and nursed her coffee.

"You'll never know if you don't try," Hattie coaxed.

"Did you know the town knew about everything?" Cora deflected the question.

"It's a small town, Bug. Everybody knows everyone else's business."

"I don't like it."

"Well, you might learn to like it."

"Learn to like everyone knowing every single thing I do? Not a chance. What if I go to school on Monday and everyone stares? How do I not have a panic attack if that happens?"

Cora felt herself start to sink into the darkness that pulled her panic front and center. She took deep breaths to steady herself and fight it off. Closing her eyes, she breathed in and out. Stress was a big factor in setting her off.

Her grandmother stroked the short locks of her hair. "Just breathe, Bug. Breathe through it."

It took her a few minutes, and thankfully no one but the staff saw, but she knew it would get around. She hated that she had these stupid attacks. Hated it.

"Let's go, sweetheart. I'll get you home, and you can go back to bed. Maybe a nap will do you some good."

She didn't mention Reed again, and neither did Cora. An outing was out of the question. As much as she wanted to go, she couldn't.

CHAPTER 9

*C*ora spent the rest of the weekend holed up in the cottage, binging on Netflix and pizza. She hid from Reed, from the prying eyes of the town, and from her Gran, who seemed to grow more worried about her by the day.

She was depressed and anxious. Riddled with guilt and anger. Half the time she felt so lost, she wondered what it would be like to just go to sleep and never wake up. She knew all this negativity wasn't good for her, and she hoped this shrink would be able to help. Thinking about herself dying scared her, but those thoughts wouldn't go away.

As much as she loved her grandmother, she missed her family. She kept thinking her mom was going to come waltzing through the door carrying grocery bags, or that her dad was going to yell for her to help him with something. Or that her little brother was going to flop down and demand she play *Black Ops* with him.

She missed them so much.

Being here without them was the hardest thing she'd faced in her seventeen years.

And she wasn't sure how much more pain she could go through.

Which was why she found herself staring at her closet, debating whether she should try to convince her gran that she'd be better served by homeschooling. The thought of all those prying eyes staring at her, judging her . . . it freaked her out.

She didn't know anyone.

Except for Reed. Whom she'd totally blown off. He'd probably not even speak to her.

There was a knock on her door, and her gran opened it, holding a cup of coffee, which Cora took gratefully.

"Nervous?"

"Do I have to go? Can't we just like homeschool me or something? I could help at the store full time."

"Store's not even open yet, and you need to go to school. Socialize, flirt, take down some mean girls. You need normal right now, Cora, more than you need to hide in your room all day."

"Fine."

She pulled out her favorite jeans and a light blue sweater she'd pull over a tank. Her new boots completed the outfit. At least she'd be warm.

It took her longer than usual to get ready because she fussed with her hair and makeup. Her mom always said makeup was a shield from the world. No matter what you might be feeling, put on your best face. It made dealing with everything easier. You might not have confidence, but you could fake it with good makeup.

She needed all the help she could get.

Her grandmother dropped her off at the high school a few minutes before classes started. She'd gotten her locker assignment when she registered, but she didn't bother with that. She had nothing to put in there. Her ID and some cash were tucked away in her book bag.

The school was just as quaint as the town with its three-story red brick structure. Any other time, she'd be enthralled with the architecture, but she was too nervous. She dug out her schedule and looked around, feeling overwhelmed.

It was a weird schedule. In Charleston, they'd had the same classes every day, but here class schedules changed depending on the day of the week. Not that she minded; it was just a lot when she was new.

"Hey!"

Cora jumped at the sound of the bright voice. She turned to see a girl standing behind her, her blond hair shining in the early morning sunshine. Bright blue eyes stared back at her.

"You look a little lost."

"I guess I am. I'm new, and I have no idea of where I'm going."

"I'm Celeste Long."

"Cora Hartwood."

"Well, Cora Hartwood, let me see your schedule, and I'll help you find your class."

"Thanks." Cora handed it to her, and she looked it over.

"Oh, we have biology together!"

"It'll be nice to at least walk in and know one person."

"Yeah, being new has to feel weird, huh?"

"Weird isn't the word for it."

"I bet. Looks like you have Spanish with Mr. Fernandez. I can show you where it is."

"Thanks. I appreciate it."

"I love your hair."

"I wasn't sure how it would go over here. I'm from South Carolina, and lots of people have strange hair colors."

"You'll fit right in," Celeste assured her. "We have just as many people here with all shades of hair."

Cora followed her into the school, and they chatted about hair as Celeste led her to the right classroom. She then gave her directions to all her other classes through lunch.

"I'll see you in biology and good luck!"

I'm going to need it, Cora thought, as she watched Celeste walk off toward her own class.

The morning passed fairly quickly, and while people did stare, there were no whispers or fingers pointing. Several people talked to her, and she hoped a few of them would turn into friends, including

Celeste, who reminded her of her own best friend, Emily. She was confident and not afraid to say what she wanted.

It was in the last period of the day that she saw Reed. He came into the room, his gaze sweeping over everyone and settling on her. That charming smile of his appeared, and he strode over, taking the seat right beside her.

"Hey, Shortcake." His deep voice sent a thrill of shivers cascading over her skin. "How'd your first day go?"

"Not as bad as I thought it would, honestly."

"Awesome. I looked for you at lunch, but I got snagged by some friends before I found you."

"That's okay. I had lunch with Celeste Long and some of her friends. They liked my hair too."

"Celeste is a cool girl." He pulled his book out of his backpack, along with a notebook. "You want a ride home or did you drive?"

"Uh . . . Gran dropped me off." He was actually talking to her. She thought for sure he'd be mad about her not calling.

"Cool, I'll take you home. Hope you don't mind if we grab some pizza first. I'm starved."

The thought of pizza caused her stomach to turn. She'd binged pizza all week.

He quirked a brow at her expression.

"Let's just say pizza is not my first choice right now."

"You got something against pizza?"

She shook her head. "It's what I ate all weekend while I binged *Stranger Things* and *House on Haunted Hill*."

"So that's what you were up to."

"I . . ."

She was saved from having to answer when the teacher called them all to attention. But through the entire class, she barely paid any attention to the lecture going on.

Instead, she focused on Reed sitting right beside her and his offer of a ride and food.

And the butterflies that refused to calm down in her stomach.

CHAPTER 10

*R*eed drove a red Chevy Blazer. It made sense, considering they were in Colorado. Cora threw her book bag in the back seat and climbed into the SUV. It was a newer model, and it was clean inside. Most guys she knew took care of their vehicles religiously.

Reed got in, buckled his seat belt, and turned on the heat. It only took a moment for warm heat to begin to blow out of the vents, and Cora held her hands up. Colorado was cold. Even bundled up in her coat and boots, she was freezing.

"You'll get used to the cold." Reed adjusted the vents so they were all pointing directly at her.

"I don't know about that. I lived in Charleston, South Carolina. We got the occasional snow flurry and the temperature could dip down pretty low sometimes, but it was never this cold this early."

"We're expecting snow tonight." His eyes twinkled when he said that.

"Snow?"

"You did just say you got snow in South Carolina, didn't you?"

"Very rarely, and when we did, it shut the whole city down."

Reed laughed. "Not here. We're used to it. Don't worry, though.

If it snows tonight, I'll come pick you up so your grandmother doesn't have to get out on the slick roads."

"Why are you being so nice to me?"

"Do you always question people's motives when they're nice to you?" He backed out of his parking spot and then drove out of the school lot and onto the street.

"You barely know me, so I just . . . I don't understand."

"You looked like you needed a friend, so I'm offering myself up as a friend."

A myriad of emotions assaulted Cora, and she pushed them down enough to talk. "Thank you, Reed."

"No worries, Shortcake. Not everyone in this town has an agenda."

"What do you mean?"

He licked his lips and glanced at her. "Why did you guys move here?"

"My gran has a friend here, Saundra something or other, and she talked my gran into it."

"Saundra Beaumont?"

"I think so." She frowned, trying to remember. "Anyway, she offered and here we are."

Reed was quiet while they drove basically across the street and pulled into the parking lot of Burger Bar. It was already packed, considering Reed had to drive around twice before he found a parking spot. It looked like the students had fled the school and flooded here.

"Is this a drive-in restaurant?" Cora asked, excited. She'd seen this kind of place on TV, and she knew Sonic of course, but this had a more authentic feel than Sonic. A lot of people had gathered outside around the stalls, and waitresses on roller skates delivered food to the occupants. She saw a guy leaning against a car filch a fry from the basket and the girl in the driver's seat mock stab him with a pencil. It was the coolest thing ever.

"Do you want to order out here and eat in the car?"

Cora was tempted, but it was too cold. "Maybe when it's warmer."

"Come on, Shortcake, let's get you and me both fed."

"Do they have milkshakes?"

"Best in town."

The inside was very retro with a black-and-white checkered floor. Booths and metal tables took up most of the floor, but there was a large counter with stools as well. Reed led her over to one of the booths in front of a large window so she could see outside.

"I love this place!"

Reed just smiled at her obvious excitement. He handed her a menu that was tucked behind the napkin dispenser.

She'd barely opened it when the waitress came by. Reed ordered a double bacon cheeseburger, fries, and a Mountain Dew. Cora decided to get a regular cheeseburger, tots, and a strawberry milkshake.

Reed chuckled.

"What?"

"Strawberry milkshake?"

"I like strawberries."

"Maybe I should call you Strawberry Shortcake then."

"Don't you dare. I'm still not sure I like the nickname Shortcake."

"You like it."

"How do you know?"

He only smiled.

"I'm sorry I didn't call you on Saturday. I wasn't up to going out."

"That's cool." He leaned back and threw his legs up beside her on the seat. "I ended up taking an extra shift on Saturday anyway. Xandru needed help fixing some plumbing. I would have called, but I didn't have your number."

Well, at least now she didn't feel so bad about not calling. He had to work anyway.

Reed cleared his throat. "That was a direct hint there, Shortcake."

"What?" She glanced up to see him shaking his head, smiling.

"Your phone number, Cora. That was me asking for your number."

"Oh." She got a little flabbergasted, those same deer in the headlights feelings she'd gotten the first time she met him rushing back.

He fished his phone out of his pocket and tossed it to her.

"What if I don't want to give you my number?"

"You do."

"Are you always this confident in your own charm?"

"Yup."

She laughed, picked up the phone, and added her number to his contacts.

"See?" he teased when he took the phone back. "You wanted to give me the number."

Cora was completely charmed, and for the first time in weeks, she didn't feel guilty for being a little happy. It had more to do with the boy sitting across from her than her healing. He put her at ease even as he made her tongue-tied. It was weird, but her life was so out of control, she'd take weird and be glad of it.

"So how ya been, Shortcake?" He tilted his head, and the sun picked out lighter colors in his dark brown hair. "You doing okay?"

"Didn't we do this already?"

"Nope, we talked about school. I meant how are you doing after everything and moving to a new town. You handling things okay?"

"Can I ask you something?"

He nodded. "Sure."

"Did you . . . did you feel guilty after your brother died?"

He sucked in a breath, and a shadow passed through his eyes.

"Every day. Still do some days. It doesn't feel right, me being here without him."

"I was supposed to be in the car, but I blew them off to go to a party. I keep thinking that if I'd been there, maybe I could have done something to save my brother, shielded him or something."

The waitress came back with their food before Reed could answer, but she could see how serious his eyes had become.

Cora took a long pull on the straw of her milkshake to avoid looking at Reed. She wasn't sure why she'd told him that. She barely knew him, for Pete's sake. No, that was a lie. She'd told him because he'd lost a brother, and Reed was her age. Not some therapist who didn't understand how her teenage brain was processing the grief of losing her entire family. Reed did, though.

"Shortcake, look at me."

Cora looked up. His expression was full of empathy.

"I can't tell you that you being in that car would have made a difference or that you might have died too. Nobody knows that, but what I do know is that you're here now and you can only control the situation in front of you. My mom says everything happens for a reason. What that reason might be is for you to discover. I'm not going to tell you how to feel, but I will tell you the same thing my mom said to me. Would your brother be happy knowing how you're torturing yourself? Would your parents? Or would they want you to try to find some kind of happiness where you can get it?"

"You're a real Dr. Phil, huh?"

He snorted. "Please. He's got nothing on all this." Reed swept his hand around himself. "Seriously, though, the guilt is a part of grieving. Just don't let it suck you down so far you can't come back."

"It's hard some days. So hard."

"Tell you what, Shortcake, when you get to that dark place, you call me. Day or night, even if you think I'm at work, in class, or asleep. You call, and we'll talk for as long as you need to."

"You barely know me."

"I have a feeling about you, Cora Hartwood. Now eat your food before it gets cold."

Cora dutifully tossed a tot in her mouth, feeling more at ease than she had since right before the sheriff showed up at the Halloween party.

They chatted about movies and music until they'd finished their food, and then Reed drove her home, promising to pick her up in the morning if it snowed.

CHAPTER 11

*I*t had been a week since Cora started school. Reed came and picked her up every day, since it had snowed for three days straight, and brought her home.

It was Saturday, and she rolled out of bed at ten a.m. because it was Saturday and she refused to get up until a decent hour. She ran to the bathroom and took a quick shower.

Her wardrobe was sorely lacking, though, so she put her pajamas back on. She found her grandmother in the kitchen looking at something on her laptop.

"Gran?"

Hattie jumped about half a foot when Cora spoke and slammed the laptop shut. Instant suspicion. That's what that little action inspired.

"What were you looking at?"

"Nothing." Hattie ran a hand through her short hair.

"Grandma, don't lie to me, please. I'm not six anymore."

Hattie let out a long sigh. "I don't want to worry you."

"Gran, not telling me is going to make me worry more. What were you looking at?"

Hattie reluctantly opened the laptop and turned it so Cora could see.

"I was going through emails and found this. It's from the woman who . . . who took them from us."

Cora blinked several times, her panic starting to rise. She took several deep breaths. "What does it say?" She couldn't bring herself to look.

"It's another threat. She wants the box opened."

"And if we don't?"

"Then she'll take you from me too."

"But she can't find us here, can she?" Cora felt the panic crawling up her spine, wrapping around her throat.

"I don't think so. I'm going to speak with Saundra this morning about it. Do you want anything from the Broastful Brew?"

"What's that?" Her voice sounded distant.

"Another coffee shop." Hattie got up and hugged her tight. "It's okay, Bug-a-boo. No one's going to hurt you. I promise."

"You're sure she can't find us here?"

"If she manages to get into Havenwood Falls, they'll know immediately. Like I told you before, there are protections in place. Do you need your pills?"

Cora nodded, hating that she did.

Hattie sat her down at the table and closed the laptop before going into Cora's room to bring her back her medicine. She swallowed the tablet and sat there, taking deep breaths. Her gran sat with her until the medicine started to work and she began to calm down.

"I'm sorry, Gran. I hate that this happens to me."

"Don't be sorry, Buggy. Your first appointment with the therapist is on Monday. I think that's going to help more than anything. You need to talk to someone about how you're feeling."

Cora wasn't looking forward to it. She didn't want to discuss her feelings. She didn't want to admit the things she thought about. Reed was helping. He never asked her to talk about her feelings, but just his being there seemed to make her feel calmer, more at peace.

"Maybe I should cancel my breakfast with Saundra."

"No, don't do that, Gran. I'll be fine. I'm already feeling better."

"I don't know . . ."

"Go. Your friend might be able to help with that woman."

"Are you sure?"

"Yes. I'm not going to do anything but laze on the couch and watch Netflix all day anyway."

Her gran didn't look convinced, but she did finally leave. Cora was slightly worried because it was snowing and the roads were still a little icy, but her grandmother handled it like a pro, as she proved when they went to the grocery store. Still, given she'd lost her family to a car crash, she worried.

After getting herself a bowl of cereal, she plopped down on the couch and turned on Netflix. She had her laptop hooked to the TV and a Beats speaker hooked to the laptop. She settled on *The Santa Clarita Diet*. It looked funny.

A knock at the door interrupted her halfway through the first episode. Thoughts of the email her gran had received were front and center, so she approached the door warily. She peeked out the window and saw Reed standing on the porch. What was he doing here?

She opened the door and then slammed it in his face, realizing she hadn't even brushed or dried her hair yet. Oh God, he'd seen her in her rattiest pajamas too.

He knocked again.

"What?"

"It's rude to slam a door in your friend's face," he said though the door. He didn't sound mad, though. More like amused.

"I, uh . . ."

"Open the door, Shortcake. I don't care what you're wearing."

She closed her eyes, embarrassed. Why did this sort of thing always happen to her?

Shaking her head, she opened the door. No point in trying to run back to her room and change. He'd already seen her.

His green eyes were laughing even if he'd schooled his expression. "You got plans today?" he asked.

"Uh . . . just Netflix. I'm not up to going out."

He nodded. "Thought you might say that, so I brought the day to you." He turned and pointed to where his SUV was parked. A girl and a guy stood there. He motioned for them to come over.

"What are you up to?"

"You are going to experience your first real snow the right way."

"I'm a beach girl, Reed. Snow and I don't mix."

"You say that now." His eyes twinkled with mischief. "But before the day is up, you are going to be a snow girl."

Cora highly doubted that.

"Cora, this is my twin sister Molly and my best friend, Henry Cole. Guys, this is Shortcake."

"So you're the one who's been stealing all my brother's time." The girl had the same laughing green eyes and dark brown hair as Reed. She was shorter than Reed, but taller than Cora.

"Don't we have a few classes together?" Cora asked to keep from answering that question.

"You're in all of my morning classes." Molly swept past her and into the cottage. "Ohhh, you're watching *The Santa Clarita Diet*. Shame they canceled it. It was funny."

Cora moved aside so Reed and Henry could come in. Henry's super short blond hair was styled and showed off his blue eyes. He looked around curiously, and Cora once again became conscious of how many boxes were strewn around. The moving van had arrived a few days ago, and while most everything was put into storage, several boxes made it inside. Her bedroom was littered with them too.

"I always wondered what these cottages looked like on the inside." Henry moved around the boxes like they weren't even there. "Cozy."

Cramped was more like it. Not that there wasn't enough room for her and her gran; the boxes just made it feel like that. She made a note to unpack as many as she could and push the rest into a corner.

Molly flopped down onto the couch and hit play on the laptop. "Well, don't just stand there. We got movies to watch."

"I'll just go get dressed."

"And comb your hair?" Reed asked, a smile playing with his lips.

She died a little inside. He'd caught her looking her worst.

He laughed at her expression. "Go on, Shortcake. Put on warm clothes. We're not going to be inside all day."

That gave her pause. She wasn't sure going outside was such a good idea, especially after the email her gran got. Instead of letting them see her panic start to rise again, she fled to her bedroom.

She'd stood him up last week, and he came to her this weekend. If she wasn't so worried, she'd be grinning like a fool, but she was scared. What if that crazy lady found her way here? What if she decided to stop waiting and just kidnap Cora? She was freaking out.

Twenty minutes later, she was still standing in the middle of her room, the what-if's going round and round in her head. If it wasn't for the anxiety medication she'd taken right before they'd arrived, she'd be a mess right now. Small blessing, that, but she'd take it.

She did the squeak scream she laughed at other girls for doing when someone knocked on her door.

"You okay in there, Shortcake?"

No, no she wasn't.

"Cora?" Reed knocked again when she didn't answer him.

"I . . ." She cleared her throat. "I'll be out in just a minute."

"Thought maybe you went back to bed on us."

"No." She forced a laugh. "Just trying to find clean clothes."

Cora yanked on a pair of jeans and pulled on a short-sleeved shirt. She found her SCU sweatshirt and added it before quickly blow-drying her hair. Venturing back out into the main room was easier with a semblance of normalcy now that her wet hair wasn't all over the place.

She really wished she hadn't when she saw Molly holding the small wooden box that held a trapped demon like it was the holy grail.

Three pairs of curious eyes nailed her to where she stood. Her grandmother's warning that this town was full of supernatural creatures, some of them probably not as friendly, came roaring back.

She'd wondered all week if Reed was one of those creatures.

Molly knew what that trap was. Cora knew it as well as she knew she herself was terrified of spiders.

And that wasn't good.

She slammed her bedroom shut again.

CHAPTER 12

"Cora, open the door." Reed's calm voice drifted to her from the other side.

What if they were working with the crazy lady?

But Reed had been so nice . . .

Of course he had. He'd been trying to get on her good side so she wouldn't suspect he was up to no good.

That's stupid, though, she told herself. She was overreacting because of that email.

"I'm good here. Why don't you guys go home? I don't feel so well."

"You're good, but you don't feel well?"

"Pretty much."

Reed said something to the others, and then she heard footsteps and the front door opening and closing.

"Okay, Shortcake, it's just you and me."

That didn't make her feel any better.

"I'm not leaving until you come out here and talk to me."

Cora closed her eyes and bowed her head. She heard the stubborn tone in his voice. He wouldn't leave until she talked to him. Getting what little courage she had left together, she straightened her spine and opened the door.

Reed was leaning against the wall right beside the door, and when she stepped out, it brought her so close, she could feel the heat radiating off him. And despite her trepidation, those danged butterflies came back.

"What's going on?" Reed asked, concerned.

Cora moved farther into the living room, her eyes looking for the box. She found it sitting on the mantel where her grandmother had put it. At least they hadn't taken it.

She turned to face him with all the bravado she could muster. "You tell me."

He studied her in that intense way of his, giving nothing away. "Why did you and your grandmother come here, Cora? Specifically here to Havenwood Falls, and don't tell me the same BS you did before. Tell me the truth."

"What makes you think it was BS?"

"The demon trap on your mantel."

Cora sucked in a breath. She was right. He did know exactly what it was. She started to slowly back away from him, and he frowned.

"Shortcake?"

"Stay where you are." She started looking for her phone, but then remembered it was charging beside her bed. Reed stood between her and her bedroom.

"Do you think I'm going to hurt you?" He sounded bewildered.

"You know what that thing is, don't you?" She asked to make sure she'd heard him right.

He nodded. "Almost anyone who deals in any kind of magic would understand what it is."

"What are you? A witch or something?"

"No. I'm as human as you can get."

"Then how . . ."

"My family deals in alchemy. We combine magic and science together to create things and find unorthodox solutions. Alchemy created that box, or don't you know that?"

She shook her head.

"How can you not know?"

"Because I'd never seen that thing until my gran showed it to me our first night here."

"Did she tell you about Havenwood Falls' secret before or after she showed you the box?"

Cora didn't know what to do. Should she trust him and confide in Reed? Just a minute ago she was thinking he was in cahoots with the crazy lady.

"I don't know what to do, who to trust."

"Have I done or said anything but be your friend?"

"No, but what if you're working with her?"

"Her?"

Cora let out a frustrated sound and sat down. If he attacked, he attacked. She was too tired for this.

He approached her like one would a wild animal—slow and with his hands held out to show her he meant no harm. He sat down in front of her on the coffee table.

"I'm not going to hurt you, Cora. I promise."

Her shoulders slumped. She was so tired, and her heart ached. She needed to trust someone, and Reed had been kind. He was right. He'd done nothing but be her friend. She couldn't let her own fears and anxieties rule her every thought and action.

"Can I trust you?"

His eyes turned solemn. "You can."

She searched his eyes, and she found nothing but truth there. And deep down she did trust him, even if she'd had a freak-out moment. Something about him sparked a deep-seated trust inside of her.

So she blurted out her truth.

"My family didn't die by accident. They were murdered."

Reed's eyes widened.

"I didn't know until we came here. Gran was in such a rush after the funeral to get us packed up and on the road. I thought it was just to get me away from all the memories. My anxiety attacks were so bad that first week."

"Anxiety attacks?" Reed took her hand and gently rubbed his thumb back and forth over the back of it. It soothed her more than almost anything else. Lulled her even. Or at least that's what she told herself.

"I was supposed to be in that car, but I blew them off to go to a party."

"And you've been blaming yourself." Reed nodded. "The what-if game will screw with your head, Shortcake."

"Every time I think of them too long, I start to panic. Gran took me to my family doctor, and she prescribed me anxiety meds. They work. I took one earlier when we got the email, or I'd be having one right now."

"I'm sorry, Cora. We have a good therapist here in town. I had to talk to her after my brother died. It helped me a lot."

"Gran has an appointment set up for me, but I don't know if I want to go or not. The thought of talking about my feelings with a stranger is weird."

"I get it, but I still think you should go. She helped me, and I think she can help you too, if you let her."

Time to change the subject. "Back to why we left. I thought it was because of my panic attacks. I couldn't even walk into my brother's room without breaking down. Gran told me about Havenwood Falls and that we were moving here instead of her home in Florida. I didn't even question it when she said we both needed a new start. It wasn't until we were almost here that she said we were running."

"Running?"

"She wouldn't explain anything until we got here. Then she told me my family makes demon traps. That my father had trapped a particularly nasty fire demon in that box on the mantel, the boyfriend of a witch. She caused the accident that took my family and then she threatened my life. That's why Gran came here. She said the town has protections that we can't get anywhere else."

"She's right. There's a spell around this town that will alert the people who need to know when another supernatural enters it.

There are rules. They have to register when they come in, and if they don't, then they're dealt with. You're safer here than anywhere else."

"I thought so, but Gran got an email this morning demanding I open the box and free him or she's going to kill me. It's why I had to take my meds. I had a panic attack."

"Do any of the people in charge here know about these threats?" Reed asked, keeping up his gentle massage on her hand.

"Gran has been talking to her friend Saundra."

"Saundra will get to the bottom of it."

"I don't know. At first I didn't believe any of it, but my gran wouldn't lie to me. It's just so surreal."

"If your dad made demon traps, how is it you didn't know?"

"Because apparently the men in my family are still living in the dark ages. Only the male members of the family were ever told anything about this. My gran only knows because Grampa was a man of the times and supported women's rights."

"All the women in my family are part of our alchemy heritage. It blows my mind it was kept from you."

"I wish it still was, honestly. I liked my average life full of nothing but friends and parties and living blissfully in ignorance of the supernatural world."

"It's rough, having everything you thought you knew ripped away from you right after everything that happened. It takes some getting used to, but the supernaturals here are just like us humans in the respect that they're still people. They have feelings, and some of my good friends are supernatural. Don't judge them based on something you've read or seen on TV."

"Maybe you're right."

"I am right." He winked. "You need to stop worrying so much. If Saundra knows, then those who need to be on the lookout are."

"I guess." She'd worry no matter what.

"Now, go grab your coat. We've got stuff to do."

"I don't know . . . What if . . ."

"What did I just say about what-ifs?"

"They'll drive you crazy."

"Exactly, Shortcake. Get your coat. I'm going to show you the magic of snow."

"Uh, no. I'm perfectly content to admire it from here."

He laughed. "Come on. It'll be fun. I promise."

"You make a lot of promises, Reed Spencer."

"And I always keep them. Coat."

Begrudgingly, she got up and pulled on her boots and her coat. If he so much as threw a snowball at her . . .

CHAPTER 13

"Duck!"

Cora dived for the ground beside Molly as a volley of snowballs whizzed over her head. Henry and Molly hadn't left as she thought. They'd just walked to the square to get coffee before coming back.

"Henry is lethal with a snowball," Molly whispered as she and Cora huddled behind their makeshift fort.

Considering he'd nailed her twice in the space of twenty seconds, Cora agreed. Reed's aim was good, but Henry's was professional-sports-worthy.

"I have a plan," Molly went on as she started shaping snowballs.

"Good, because I don't," Cora muttered. "Take me to the beach and I can win a sandcastle competition without trying, but anything that involves snow flying at my face and I'm worthless."

Molly laughed. "Just keep making these things and leave the rest to me." Her green eyes danced with mischief. "Henry is going down."

"He likes you, you know."

"What? No, he doesn't."

"He does." Cora smiled slyly as she formed snowballs. Reed had been right when he said this would help to relax her a little. She'd all but forgotten her worries from earlier, at least for a little while. "I've seen him watching you when he thinks no one else is looking."

"You mean the way my brother watches you?" Molly shot her a cheeky grin.

"We're friends."

"Uh huh. I give you another week before he kisses you."

A little thrill went through her at the thought of Reed's lips on hers, but she shoved it down. She had other things to worry about.

"Nice try changing the subject, but you like Henry as much as he likes you. Is Reed the problem?"

Molly huffed. "I do like him, but I don't think he likes me. Besides that, you're right about Reed. I don't know what he'd think if I went out with his best friend since before kindergarten."

"He'd get over it."

Molly snorted. "He once held a grudge against me for over a year because I broke his Transformers toy when we were little."

Molly raised up enough to peek out over the wall of snow that barely counted as a wall. A dozen snowballs came hurtling toward her, and she all but fell back down.

"You really have a plan to get by that?"

"I do." Molly surveyed their haul of snowballs. "Get ready."

Cora grabbed as many as she could hold and waited.

"Here, Fluffy, Fluffy, Fluffy."

Fluffy?

There was an immediate reaction from across the way. The boys started shouting.

And Molly stood and started slinging snowballs at them. Cora did the same, unsure of why a cat would terrify the boys, but she threw the snowballs as best she could. When Molly shouted for them to make a run for it, she took off running for the front door of the cottage, dodging around the snowmen they'd built before the epic snowball fight.

Just as they slammed the door, they heard the thudding of countless snowballs hit the wood.

"We win!" Molly sang through the door.

"You ran!" Henry shouted. "That means you forfeit."

"Nope. We hit you guys with the most snowballs."

"You cheated!"

"I used a weakness to my advantage, so suck it up boys and go get us some pizza."

There was some grumbling, but they left to do as Molly bid.

"Why are they so afraid of a cat?"

"Because it's not a cat." Molly laughed so hard she bent over.

"What is it then?"

"A skunk who sprays Henry every time she sees him. She's a pet of a little old lady who lives near here, and the skunk roams free most days."

A skunk? Cora laughed, picturing the two boys climbing up onto anything they could to escape the stinky little black-and-white creature.

Peeling off her gloves and coat, she turned the heat up a little to thaw them out. If she could have started a fire, she would have, but she was not outdoorsy at all and she lumped wood-burning fireplaces in with outdoor activities.

"You want something to drink? We have water and Mountain Dew."

"Nectar of the gods, Mountain Dew."

Cora grabbed them each a can of pop and then came back over to the couch, her eyes going to the now-empty mantel. She'd put the demon trap in her gran's room. Out of sight, out of mind. Didn't really work that way, but it helped her pretend it didn't exist. At least for right now.

"So, what do you think of our little town?"

"It's beautiful."

"But?" Molly prompted.

"I miss the city. Charleston wasn't huge, but I could find any restaurant or big box retailer I liked within five minutes of where I lived. And it wasn't as quiet as it is here. I think the quiet is what takes so much getting used to."

"I've never lived anywhere but here." Molly's expression turned disgruntled. "We drive in to some of the bigger cities near here that have the big box retailers, and we've gone to Walt Disney World and a few other places for vacation, but we can't be gone more than a month from home and that bites."

"The memory spell."

Molly nodded. "Yeah. I can't even go away to school, because I'll forget everyone. I love my home. I love Havenwood Falls, but sometimes . . ."

"Sometimes it feels restrictive and unnecessarily harsh?"

"Exactly. I want to travel. I want to see New York City and go to Europe and do a lot of things, but I can't if it'll take longer than the allotted twenty-eight days."

"Can't they make an exception or something?"

"No. The rules are there for a reason, and they keep us all safe."

"The thought of losing my gran after losing everyone else is . . . it scares me. I guess if Gran puts down roots here, then so will I."

"I'm sorry about your family. I didn't want to mention it before because, well, Reed thought you needed distracting from it. The goal was to make you laugh today."

A soft smile graced Cora's lips. "He's a really good guy."

"Yeah, he is, and he really likes you, so don't make me pull my B-switch out if you hurt him. I like you, and I'd hate to do that, but I would."

"Reed has been nothing but nice to me even when he gets a little cocky, so if I ever hurt him, you have my permission to flip that switch."

"I knew I liked you for a reason." Molly grinned. "So, you really think Henry likes me? He usually treats me like the little sister he never had."

"Girl, please. That boy can't keep his eyes to himself."

"He did just break up with his girlfriend." Her voice turned thoughtful. "Maybe I'll corner him and make a move. If I wait for him to do it, I'll be eighty with ten snotty grandkids."

"You should. No one says you have to wait for him to man up."

"Right? Reed can just get over it if he has an issue. Or maybe you can distract him for me." She wiggled her eyebrows suggestively.

"I'm not in the right place for a boyfriend right now. I'm still dealing with stuff."

"That's cool, but Reed's patient. He'll wait until you are ready because he really likes you."

"He's just being a good friend."

"Please. You are all he's talked about since he met you. Reed has never acted like this about any girl. It's why I demanded to meet you. I could have introduced myself, but he swore me off. He didn't want to freak you out, all things considered."

"Really? He talks about me?"

"If I heard your name one more time, I might have resorted to supergluing his mouth shut."

Cora's stomach got all fluttery, and a warm glow started to burn away some of the unbearable pain she'd been in for weeks. Not so much that it took the pain away, but it dulled just a little.

"I'm notorious for spoiling movies, so let's find something else to watch until the guys get back with the pizza." Molly leaned back and took ownership of the remote control and Cora's laptop. "What are you in the mood for?"

"Something the guys will groan about having to watch."

"I like the way you think." Molly grinned and started looking through Netflix.

Cora sat back and let her pick out the movie, content and a little better than she had been since her family died.

And that was all because of Reed Spencer.

CHAPTER 14

"Gran, have you seen the box with all my books in it?"

Hattie looked up from the TV. She'd become addicted to *iZombie*. "It's in your room. I saw it yesterday."

Cora was in the mood to read, and her favorite series was *Chronicles of Nick* by Sherrilyn Kenyon. She owned every single copy in hardback. The urge to get lost in that world tonight was strong, so she'd gone to look for her book box.

Going back into her room, Cora rummaged in the boxes she'd piled up in the corner. After everyone had left, she spent the rest of the afternoon cleaning the boxes up.

Of course the box she wanted was on the very bottom. Sighing, she moved them until she'd unearthed the box and dragged it over to her bed. Books were heavy, so she didn't even try to lift it up. The foot of her bed would be its new home until they moved into the apartment over the store.

Eyeballing the mess she'd made, Cora decided to worry about it tomorrow. Instead, she pulled the packing tape away and started piling books out, looking for the series. Her hand closed around a small white box with a red ribbon around it. Her name was written on the gift tag in her mother's handwriting.

She sat down on the floor and held the package like it was the most precious thing in the world, and in a way, it was. At least to her. How had it gotten into her books? She didn't remember putting it in there, but she wasn't the only person who'd packed her room up. Emily had come over to help. Maybe she'd put it in there, thinking Cora would find it later when she was ready for it.

This was the last thing her mother had ever gotten her.

She set the box gently on the floor and stared at it. It must have been a Christmas present. She traced the outline of the red ribbon almost reverently. Could she open it without a panic attack rising up?

Her hand started to shake when she pulled the ribbon and slid it off. Slow deep breaths, she reminded herself. It took her a minute, but the shaking stopped, and she was able to lift the lid of the box.

A dark black velvet jewelry box lay nestled amongst the white tissue paper. She picked it up and opened it, a gasp falling from her lips.

Inside she found a necklace with a crescent moon and star design. She used to read to the man in the moon when she was little, telling her mom that even the man in the moon needed a bedtime story. Her mom must have seen this and remembered it.

It was sterling silver because she was allergic to gold. Little diamonds were scattered throughout the interlocking pieces of the moon and star, making it sparkle in the light. It was such a thoughtful gift.

Cora lifted it out of the box and latched it around her neck. Tears trickled down her cheeks, falling unabashedly. This would be a gift she cherished—

Pain lanced her skin all at once, and she screamed. The place where the pendant lay against her skin felt like it was on fire. She tried to pull it away, but it was stuck, and she screamed again, calling for her grandmother.

Hattie ran into the room. "What's wrong?"

"It's burning, get it off, get it off, get it off!" Cora tried to pry the pendant from her skin, but it wouldn't budge.

Hattie rushed to her and tried to pry the necklace off Cora's skin, but nothing moved it. "It won't come off. Where did you get this?"

Cora pointed to the box. "It was in with the books. I thought Emily found it and put it in there."

Hattie picked up the box. "This is your mother's handwriting."

The pain increased, and she jumped up, running to the bathroom. She turned on the cold water and scooped some in her hands, then poured it over the necklace. The burn didn't waver.

"Gran, do something!" She was crying in earnest now. It really hurt.

Hattie ran out of the room and came back with her phone pressed to her ear, explaining to whoever was on the other side what was going on. She hung up a moment later.

"Saundra is on her way over. She may be able to help."

Cora tried the water again, but there was no relief to be had. She kept pulling at the pendant and then grabbed the chain and yanked hard. All that accomplished was breaking the chain. The pendant remained glued to her skin.

The burn started to spread, and she cried out as it lanced across her chest and toward her arms.

"Get in the shower, Cora." Her gran turned the cold water on, and Cora stepped into the tub, letting the ice-cold water flow over her. It didn't lessen the burn slowly spreading across her body.

"It's not helping." Cora turned her face up, letting the water hit her chest where the pendant lay. She bent over, unable to breathe because of the pain.

"I'll get the box. Open it and let him out."

Everything in her rebelled against that. She knew what it took to open the box. She'd read it in her family's journals.

"If we do that, he'll just kill us both and then go out and do God knows what to the people here in town. That's not an option, Gran."

She would never let that thing go out and kill people. Never.

Trapping that thing cost her father his life, and she would not let him have died in vain. Him, her mother, or her brother. Their lives should mean something.

Even if it meant her death, she'd keep him locked in that box.

The irony suddenly occurred to her. The demon was trapped in a white box, and her death came in the form of a white box.

Someone started pounding on the door, and her gran ran to get it. She came back followed by several women, most of whom waited just outside the bathroom door. The one directly behind Gran seemed to be in charge. Her silver hair was piled up in a twist, and her lighter jacket contrasted with the black skirt she had on. Very businesslike. She had this air about her, a sense of power and confidence. This must be Saundra Beaumont.

"Let me see."

Saundra came forward, and Cora turned to let her see the pendant, the cold water from the shower head spraying her back. Saundra held out her hand, and an intense look of concentration overtook her expression.

When she stepped back, her concern was more than apparent.

"Tell me everything that happened." Her tone wasn't overly kind, but her concern shone through, which worried Cora.

"I found it in my box of books. The box had my mom's handwriting on it. I put it on thinking it was a gift from her. It started to burn the minute it touched my skin."

"Is the cold water helping?"

Cora shook her head.

"Then there's no reason to freeze to death," Saundra said. "Hattie, get her some warm clothes while we discuss this. Your granddaughter put on a cursed object. We need to work fast before it does what it was meant to do."

"What was it meant to do?" Cora asked, stepping out of the shower.

"Kill you."

Fear rushed to the surface, but behind that fear was the thought that this thing could do exactly what she'd thought about doing for weeks. She could die. She could be with her family again. Her pain would stop. The guilt of living when they were gone would go away.

But then she looked at her grandmother.

Hattie was the reason she hadn't killed herself. It wasn't just Cora who lost everyone. Hattie had too, and killing herself would leave her gran all alone. She couldn't do that to her.

She would fight this to the bitter end.

CHAPTER 15

ora changed into a pair of flannel pajamas, and her gran
toweled her hair dry. She couldn't do it herself. Moving
hurt. It caused the burn to worsen. Walking into the living room
was a chore. The more she moved, the more the pain spread.

Saundra and the other women were huddled together when she
walked in. They looked more than troubled.

"This is a strong curse, one we can't break."

Well, she certainly got right down to business.

"But we are not going to give up hope. The fact that you're not
dead yet means the witch is hoping the pain she's causing is enough
to make you release her lover from his prison."

"I won't do that."

Saundra nodded, a little hint of respect entering her gaze. "We
are going to take the chain and see if we can use it to locate the
witch. I've seen a version of this curse before, and the caster is the
only one who can break it. We do have an alternate option I've got
people researching now, but I'm not sure it'll work."

"So I just sit here in pain until she decides to kill me or you find
a workaround?"

"Unfortunately, yes."

Great. Just freaking great. Cora took several shallow breaths when a band of pain wrapped around her chest.

"She's thought this through, going so far as to plant it before the moving van left your driveway."

"Is there any way we can trick her into thinking I'll let him out?"

"No." Saundra shook her head. "I wouldn't fall for it, and I'm not about to underestimate a woman whose sole purpose is to free the man she loves. Unless your situation becomes critical, we wait for her to contact you. She won't wait long, because that curse is fast acting, and she'll want you to free her lover before you burn up."

"Burn up?"

"The curse is designed to act like fire, burning you up from the inside out until you burst into flame."

She swallowed. Dying in a car crash was completely different than burning alive.

"We're not going to let you die, Cora," Saundra reassured her. "You have to hang in there until we can find a way to fix this."

"Is there anything you can do to dull the pain?" Hattie asked, wringing her hands, looking every bit her age in that moment. Gone was the flippant cool flighty grandma and there stood a woman who had aged in minutes.

"No. I'm sorry, Hattie."

"What can I do for her?"

"Trust that I'll fix this. We are going to work through the night, and I'll be back as soon as I have a solution. Before I leave, check to see if she emailed again."

Hattie opened her laptop and logged into her email. Her face blanched.

"She says we have two hours to release him or Cora dies. The email came through half an hour ago."

Saundra muttered something Cora couldn't hear, but she was too focused on the fact that she had an hour and a half left to live.

"I have an idea, but it's going to take time to gather the things we need. In the meantime, I think you should come with me, Hattie."

"No, I'm not leaving her here alone."

"Hattie, if I don't get back in time, then . . ." Saundra broke off and looked at Cora regretfully.

"She's right, Gran. You need to go with her." Cora understood what Saundra didn't say. If she wasn't able to fix this, then she'd burst into flames, and it could cost her grandmother her life. She wasn't about to let that happen. "I need you to be safe."

Hattie shook her head, that stubborn glint coming into her eyes.

"Please, Gran. Go with Mrs. Beaumont. If you died because of me, my soul would always be haunted. Don't make me blame myself for your death too. Please, Gran."

Her grandmother's shoulders slumped, and Cora knew she'd won. Hattie understood what all the blame Cora lived with did to her, and she wouldn't add to that pain if she could help it.

"I'm not going far. Just to the main house of the inn."

Cora smiled, biting back another scream that was welling up in her throat. The pain was starting to become unbearable. "Take the box with you, Gran, just in case."

"We'll lock it away where no one will be able to get to it." Saundra nodded to her and waited for her gran to fetch the box. "I'll be back as quickly as I can."

Cora gave her grandmother a quick hug and tried to smile. She was pretty sure it came out more of a grimace.

"I love you, Buggy."

"I love you too, Gran."

She watched them leave, and only then did she let the barest of whimpers out. She hurt more than she'd ever physically hurt in her life. And sitting here alone with nothing to do but watch the clock was torture.

The minutes ticked by as she tried to not think about anything. A half an hour came and went. Then another half an hour.

She tried again to pull the pendant from her skin, which was so hot it was starting to blister. It wouldn't budge.

Cora couldn't help but to think that maybe she deserved this for blowing off her family that night. For not being there for her little brother. It would be simple to just let go and not fight this. It would ease her guilt.

Those thoughts were not good, and she needed to shut them down. Her grandmother deserved to not lose everyone, but sitting here watching the minutes tick by wasn't helpful. She needed something to distract her from her deepest thoughts.

So she forced herself to get up and go find her phone.

Each step was excruciating. The pain radiated down her arms, her back, her stomach. By the time she returned to the couch, she had to just sit there for a few minutes and let the pain subside— either that or she got used to it.

She called Reed.

"Shortcake?"

"Hey," she whispered. "That offer to talk anytime still open?"

"Are you okay?"

"No, Reed, I'm not."

"What's wrong? Do I need to come over there? I'm at work, but I'm sure I can get off . . ."

"No. It's too dangerous to come here."

"Dangerous? What's going on?"

She told him everything from the necklace to her dark thoughts and why she was trying not to think like that.

"I'm coming down."

"No, Reed. I don't want you to get hurt."

"I won't come inside, but I'll be right in front of the cottage so you can see me, okay? You're not alone, Cora. You'll never be alone as long as I'm around."

That was the sweetest thing anyone had ever said to her.

Cora's leg shook as she pushed up off the couch. The pain had spread through all her limbs. She was so hot she had no doubt her blood was boiling. She focused on putting one foot in front of the other until she reached the window.

"You still with me, Shortcake?"

"Yes." She gripped the curtains and looked out, surprised to see a large number of people gathered outside. "There's people here, Reed."

"It's probably Saundra and members of her coven. You said they were trying to help."

She hoped they'd found a way to stop this for her grandmother's sake.

"I'm here, right outside. Can you see me?"

Cora searched the crowd and found him pushing through so he stood in front of the coven, facing her. Just seeing him wilted away some of her fear and dark thoughts about dying. Reed rooted her in the here and now. She didn't understand that until this moment.

"I see you."

"Hang on, okay? Don't give up yet. I just found you, Cora. I don't want to lose you."

"I'm trying."

A whoosh interrupted her and she turned her head to see the curtain erupt into flames where she was clutching it. The phone in her hand sizzled and started to melt. She dropped it and looked out the window, seeking Reed, horrified.

A fresh burst of pain scorched her skin, and she screamed, unable to stop herself. Flames erupted and licked her skin, racing to cover every inch of her, and she stumbled backward, the fire around her spreading as she was consumed in flame, the pain unbearable.

She glanced toward the window as she fell to her knees, but she couldn't see outside. She was alone, but she wasn't. Reed was there, and his presence gave her strength.

But even that wasn't enough to conquer a house on fire, and when one final blast of pain ripped through her, she fell backwards, her vision going dark as the fire from within and without consumed her.

CHAPTER 16

The sound of whispers reached her first.

She tried to open her eyes, but they refused.

Her body ached. Her skin tingled.

She was fuzzy.

What happened?

She searched her memory, and when those memories came back, so did the fear and the feel of the pain as the fire consumed her. It would be a memory forever etched into her skin.

Was she dead?

Maybe that was why she couldn't open her eyes and only heard whispers. Was she in the realm of the dead?

She thought she'd feel relief in death, like some weight would be lifted off her, but in truth, all she felt was regret.

Her gran was all alone now, and Reed . . .

She'd never be able to see where things would have gone with Reed. Cora suspected her mother's advice on *the one* had been right. Reed was her one. And now that chance was gone.

She thought death would be more than this, more than shadows and whispers. Weren't your loved ones supposed to greet you? Where were her parents? Her brother?

Soft, gentle fingers stroked her cheek, and she calmed, recognizing her grandmother's touch.

But that made no sense.

Her grandmother wasn't dead. She'd gone to the inn. She should have been safe from the fire.

"Shh, Buggy, you're safe."

Gran? She wasn't dead? But how was that even possible? She'd burned to death. There was no denying that simple fact.

"Open your eyes for me."

She tried again, but still no luck.

She really wasn't dead?

"Give her time, Hattie. She suffered through a horrible ordeal."

"What if you're wrong and she doesn't wake up?"

There was true fear in her grandmother's voice.

"She will."

Reed? Reed was here?

"He's right, Hattie. His sacrifice ensured she'll wake up. Let's go get a cup of coffee. Reed, you'll wait with her?"

"Yes, ma'am."

"You'll call me if she wakes up?"

"Of course." His deep voice sent a shiver through her. It seemed to affect her more now than it had before.

She heard the shuffle of feet and then nothing.

Movement to her right caught her ear's attention. She heard the scrape of a chair being dragged and then she felt him settle beside her.

"Shortcake, you need to wake up. You're scaring us all. It's been two days." He took her hand, and his thumb started rubbing back and forth across it like he had the day she told him the truth about the demon trap. It calmed her even more.

She tried to open her eyes again and managed a small slit. She could see his outline, but after a moment, she let them fall shut again. It was hard, waking up.

"When I thought I lost you, it was like I couldn't breathe. Everything in me died a little."

She understood that feeling all too well. She lived it after her family died.

"I'm still going to be your friend first, Cora, but after watching you burn up in that fire, I'm going to be more when you're ready. I'm not going to lose you again."

What did he mean, she burned up? How was she here?

"Cora?" he whispered, leaning closer. "Can you hear me? Squeeze my hand if you can."

She tried, but she wasn't sure if it worked.

"Come on, sweetheart, you can do it. Squeeze my hand."

She concentrated on the feel of his fingers wrapped around hers and tried with every ounce of strength she could muster to do what he asked.

"That's it. Open your eyes for me, Shortcake."

Cora fought hard and managed to open her eyes. Everything was blurry at first, but soon her vision cleared and she was able to see. Reed had moved from the chair to the bed, and she could see him in the stark light of the florescent lights. Her eyes were a little sensitive, but it was nothing she couldn't handle.

"There you are." He smiled, and his dimples came out of hiding. She loved those dimples.

Cora tried to speak, but nothing came out.

"Don't try to talk. Your body has to acclimate itself. It'll take a few minutes before your speech comes back."

What was he talking about?

"I know this is confusing, but I'll clear everything up. I promise."

He was always making promises to her and he had yet to break one. She'd only known him for two weeks, and yet she trusted him to keep his word, to be there.

"Are you thirsty?"

She managed a nod, and he got up to get a bottle of water. She looked around and saw that she was in a hospital room, connected to an IV machine. The tickle of the plastic oxygen cable rubbed along her nose.

He came back with an opened bottle of water and helped her drink a few sips. "Sorry it's warm."

When the water hit her tongue, her senses woke up, and her mouth felt jammed full of cottontails. She coughed, and Reed made a distressed noise. He went to set the water down, and she shook her head. She needed more water.

He frowned but let her drink more. When she tried to guzzle the water, he took it away. "Careful, you'll get sick. You've been out for two days."

"I . . ." She coughed again, her vocal chords loosening up. "Wha . . . whaaa . . ."

"What happened?" Reed asked, helping her lay back down and setting the water aside.

She nodded.

"The Luna Coven couldn't stop the curse, so they changed it."

Changed it?

"The fire was meant to destroy, but fire is cleansing too. It's a form of rebirth, so they twisted the curse so that you would be rebirthed from the flames consuming you."

That made no sense.

Reed chuckled. "I'm terrible at explaining. There is one creature that is reborn from the ashes of a fire and that's a phoenix. So they changed the curse to create a phoenix from your ashes. But there had to be a sacrifice for the spell to work. In order to bring you back, you had to have an anchor here in the world of the living, someone who keeps your ashes from floating away in the wind. Your grandmother wanted to do it, but Mrs. Beaumont didn't think she was strong enough because of her age. So I volunteered."

Her eyes widened. He volunteered?

"It means that every time you die, I age a whole day. As long as you're young, so am I. Not too much of a tradeoff. Think of me as your new protector. I'll always be here watching out for you. Told you I keep my promises."

"I . . ." Cora cleared her throat. "I . . ."

"Shh, no talking. Just listen, okay?" When Cora nodded, he

continued. "The threat to you isn't gone. That's part of why they didn't want your grandmother to anchor you. Each time you die, it steals a day of your anchor's life. Given her age, it might do more than steal a day of life. Until the witch is found and dealt with, you're still a target. A little harder to hurt now, but still a target."

No.

"You're safe here in Havenwood Falls."

She snorted at that. The crazy witch lady still managed to get to her despite all their protections.

"I know you probably don't believe it, but it's true. No one knew the depths the witch would resort to. She used something she found in your things, something that would mean more to you than your fears. That won't happen again. *I* won't let it happen."

Cora believed he'd do everything in his power to make sure that never happened again, but until the witch was found and dealt with as he'd said, she wasn't safe.

She might never be safe again.

"There are a few things that are going to change, though. You need to register with the Court of the Sun and the Moon because you're no longer quite human. You're a supernatural creature, a phoenix."

She wasn't human anymore. Cora didn't quite know how to feel about that.

"Because you're not a natural born phoenix, they're not sure what you can and can't do. Or if you'll be able to control any abilities you gain. And that puts the students at Havenwood Falls High in danger."

She didn't want to hurt anyone.

"What that means is that you'll probably move to the private school where you don't have to hide your supernatural abilities and you'll learn to use and control them. But that's only if you manifest any sort of ability. Until that happens, they may let you stay at school with me and Molly."

Cora blinked. He threw so many things at her so fast, she didn't know what to think.

"It's a lot, I know, but you have time to deal with it. You're alive, Shortcake. That's what matters. We will handle everything one day at a time. You and me, your gran and the coven. You're not alone. Never ever again will you be alone. One more promise I kept.

"I better call your gran. She's been worried about you."

Cora nodded and smiled. He was right. She wasn't alone, and she would deal with this one day at a time.

For now she would just be grateful to be alive even if that dark voice in the back of her mind said she cheated death again.

But that was a problem for another day.

She'd enjoy today and deal with the rest tomorrow.

CHAPTER 17

*C*ora Jean,

    My time is almost up, and I've worried over this since the day you were born. I know you father will raise you in the ways of Christianity, as all the women in our family are. He will not tell you about our darker history. It is the Hartwood way. Our women are kept out of the family business and their souls remain pure.

But I think it is your destiny to carry on the family business. I've watched you grow up, seen your affinity with the elements that are necessary to do the work we do. I know I'm not making sense, but I'll get to that soon enough.

You're special, baby girl. I've known it since the day you were born under the solstice moon. You are the first girl born into our family in over four hundred years—did you know that? The magic of our ways lies within you. Your father disagrees, but an old man knows what he knows. And I'll be damned if I let your father dictate to me what I know to be right.

Our family is different, our origin going back to before the Roman Empire. Hattie has promised to explain anything that you might be confused about after you read this letter and my journals. I kept nothing from her, as I knew one day she would be here when I wasn't. I wish I could be the one to help you through this, but cancer has robbed us both of that experience.

But I digress. Our family learned of the other world that lives around us, a world full of magic and dark creatures. There are truly evil creatures in the world, and our family was tasked with containing them. We learned how to use rituals, magic, and science to craft a cage of sorts for malevolent beings in spirit form. These could be anything from ghosts that have gone bad to demons that move among us through a host body. Not all demons require a host, but for the ones that do, our family knows how to keep them from hurting others. My journals detail the process for you.

I know you must be thinking your Grandpa was off his rocker. That's what your father said to me when I sat him down and explained it all. I had to show him what the traps did before he believed me. Once he understood, he took up the mantle of our cause. Learning of the horrible things that are in this world is one thing, but being able to prevent an innocent from being harmed . . . well, that's the most important part of what we do. It's a great responsibility that has been thrust upon our shoulders and one I hope you decide to carry alongside your brother. We can prevent harm, we can save people, and that is the greatest reward there is.

I have outlined in the journals the process for making the traps. They have to be made from the wood of a specific tree, a tree we have cultivated on our land in Ireland. The forest is hidden from the naked eye and tended to by our allies. Your father planted a few in the States as well and harvested wood from time to time. It is an ancient, sacred tree and has to be protected. Your grandmother has all the information you need on the property in Ireland in case your father tries to deny you access.

I wish our family didn't try to keep the women away from this. In the old days, women were seen as the weaker of the sexes, more susceptible to temptation and therefore susceptible to being manipulated by the spirits we trapped. We don't do the trapping ourselves so much anymore, but when we do, it is a hard task, one that can leave scars on *your soul. I understand wanting to keep you safe, but I think you are strong enough to do what needs to be done.*

You are special, baby girl, and it is my hope that you carry on our family tradition. It is also my hope that you bring the traditions of the old world back into this, strengthening what we've lost.

I love you, Cora Jean, and even though I am not there with you, I am in spirit.

With all my love,
Grandpa

Cora looked up from the letter her grandmother had handed her to three large journals on the foot of the hospital bed. Her grandfather had laid out his plans for her, and it seemed that no matter what she might want, fate had chosen a different path for her than she'd planned.

"I don't know what to say to any of this."

"You don't have to say anything, Buggy. Take some time and read through the journals. Look over the process of making the traps. Learn the spells and the science of it. Ask me your questions as you come to them. Then, if you decide you don't want to continue to make the traps, we'll put all this away and never think of it again."

Hattie sipped her coffee and nibbled on one of those scones she had recently been obsessed with. Just a few days before the fire, Cora had teased her she was going to break out in a blueberry pox, she ate so much of them.

"I do have a question for you, Gran, one that has been bothering me since the fire."

Hattie leaned back and set her coffee down. "What question?"

"Well, you said I was the only person who could open that box because it had to have Hartwood blood. Why would the witch kill me if I was the last Hartwood? She'd never get her boyfriend back with me dead."

"You are not the only Hartwood left, Buggy. You're forgetting your uncle, your grandfather's brother. Your great-grandfather chose your grandpa as his successor and while George never knew of the traps, his blood, and that of his sons, would still open the trap. That was the witch's last resort since we were the ones that had the box."

Cora didn't really know her great-uncle, since they lived in England. She'd only met that side of the family once, when she was little and they came to the States for a family reunion. It made sense, though, that they could open the traps and why the witch was willing to kill her. It would be another message to her uncle's family that the woman would kill anyone to get what she wanted.

"Are you and Saundra sure I'm safe here, Gran? What if the witch realizes that I'm not dead?"

"The coven is working to identify the witch. It's why they didn't immediately move the trap into a place the witch couldn't reach. They wanted to lure her here to you. Your father left very little by way of notes. We know who the demon is and they're hoping they can use that as a starting point to find the woman. In the meantime, they've decided to work a new spell into your Registry tattoo to hide you from her. No matter how many location spells she casts or who she sends to track you down, it won't work. She could pass you on the street and never realize it was you. They've also moved the trap to a place that it can't be found either."

"What do you mean, Registry tattoo?"

"Every supernatural being here in the town has to register with the Court of the Sun and the Moon, the supernatural leaders of the town. The Registry is the town's way of keeping track of everyone. All not-quite-human residents require a tattoo. Visitors are granted a temporary one. It's part of the town laws."

She remembered Reed saying something about some kind of registration, but the only thing she'd really focused on was the fact that she wasn't human anymore. She was still trying to wrap her head around it.

A tattoo, though? That she could get behind. Cora had always wanted a tattoo, and now she was being given permission to get one.

"What design?"

"Addie will be here later to ink you, so you can talk to her about what you want."

"Who's Addie?"

"She does all the town's tattoos for the Court. Now, do you have a design in mind?"

She loved the crescent moon, but that cursed necklace ruined it for her. She did have an idea, though.

"Why not a phoenix rising? This whole thing started with fire and ended with fire, but I'm going to look at it as a second chance instead of the nightmare it was. Reed said fire can mean rebirth too, so that's what I'm going with. It's a second chance for me."

"That sounds like a wonderful idea, Buggy."

"Gran, do you think it's okay to be happy even though they're gone?"

"Honey, your parents and your brother loved you. They'd want you to stop torturing yourself and be happy. It's not wrong. You can be sad and even angry because they're gone, but you can be happy to be alive too."

Cora nodded. "Think we can reschedule the therapist session? I want to be happy, Gran. Reed helps, but I do need to talk to someone. Someone who can help me to deal with their deaths, but also who can help me deal with all of this being thrust upon me. I mean, I was human one second and a fire girl the next."

"Fire girl?"

"I may have gone to the bathroom and noticed smoke coming out of the tips of my fingers last night."

Hattie frowned. "I . . ."

"I'm joking, Gran. I have no idea if I'm a fire bug or not. I don't feel any different. I don't think I've got any special powers."

"Saundra thinks once your body finishes acclimating, you might start manifesting."

"We'll worry about that when the time comes. But back to this tattoo business. You said I'd be safe from her and anyone she might send? How does that work?"

"It's a spell they crafted, like a memory spell. Anyone wishing to find you that is not a town resident will walk right past you. Only the town will know who you are."

"Huh. Witches can do that?"

"A single witch, no, but a coven of witches working together—you'd be amazed at what they can do."

"So I'm really safe?" Cora thought back to the night of the fire and how scared she'd been. She'd thought she was done for, but now that she'd been given a second chance, she wanted it. Her biggest fear was the witch realizing she wasn't dead and coming back for her. Maybe hurting Gran or Reed.

But if her gran was right and this tattoo thing worked, then she was safe. They were all safe.

"Gran, I don't want to make demon traps. At least not right now. Maybe once I'm done with college. Reed said there was a new college right here in town. I was thinking I could maybe go there or do online classes. I want to make candy and watch all the little kids' faces light up when they see me making it. I want to do so much."

Her gran picked up the journals from the hospital bed and put them back into the massive purse she was sporting. "These will always be here if and when you're ready. You be you, Cora, not who everyone else wants you to be, and life will lead you to the path you're meant to be on. It always does."

That much was true. Life would always push you to where you needed to be. Sometimes those pushes were so painful, they were debilitating, such as losing her family, but it brought her here and it brought her Reed.

Maybe one day she would make traps, but right now she wanted to be seventeen. She wanted to graduate high school and then college. She wanted to learn what it meant to be a phoenix, if anything. She needed to do all that before she thought about anything else.

And she had a feeling Havenwood Falls would help her with it and so much more.

For the first time since she lost her family, a sort of peace settled over her.

She was home.

We hope you enjoyed this story in the Havenwood Falls High series of novellas featuring a variety of supernatural creatures. The series is a collaborative effort by multiple authors.

Other books you might enjoy in the Young Adult Havenwood Falls High series:

Somewhere Within by Amy Hale
Awaken the Soul by Michele G. Miller
Avenoir by Daniele Lanzarotta
Saving Infiniti by Rose Garcia
Willful by Liz Ferry

Stay up to date at www.HavenwoodFalls.com

ABOUT THE AUTHOR

Apryl Baker is a USA Today bestselling author. She lives in a small town in West Virginia where she writes when she's not playing with her nieces and nephews.

ACKNOWLEDGMENTS

First I want to thank Kristie Cook for allowing me to create a story in her wonderful Havenwood Falls world. I fell in love with the world a few years ago when I first stumbled across the books through a friend of mine who raved about them. I was very honored to be asked to write a new Havenwood Falls High novella. She gave me a chance and I hope you all love Cora and Reed's story. Thank you, Kristie.

A huge thank you to Kay Steele for reading and giving me advice when I needed it. She is one of the few people who reads my work before the editor gets it, and her feedback is invaluable. She'll tell it to you like it is, even if it's not what you want to hear. And that is gold to an author. Thank you, Kay.

Also, I'd like to thank the readers of the Havenwood Falls series. Without you guys, there would be no reason to write more books. You keep us all working to create new characters and building on the lore of the town. You make what we do fun. So thank you all for reading.

And a big thank you to my readers. You guys never fail to show up and read my silly nonsense. You give me strength and courage even when writing has become so hard for me. Some of you who are new readers may not know that I am losing my eyesight slowly and writing has become difficult. On days when my eyes are so blurry I can barely see, I remember all the kind words and how much you all love my characters, and it keeps me out of a dark place myself. So thank you so much for everything.

And last but not least, thank you to my family. You put up with me when I'm working, and that's not easy. You make sure I'm fed so I don't go days without eating when I get lost in a story. I appreciate all you do for me and I love you.